Lessons Learned from the Other Side

Grief Resolution through the Use of Mediums
for Connecting to the Other Side Spirits

Barbara Ann Caruso, RN, Ph.D.

LESSONS LEARNED FROM THE OTHER SIDE
GRIEF RESOLUTION THROUGH USE OF MEDIUMS
FOR CONNECTING TO THE OTHER SIDE SPIRITS

Editors:
Konnie McCaffree, Ph.D. and Laura Bietman, MS
Sue Eckert, Contributing Editor/Reviewer
Lauvel Wooding, Editor/Reviewer

iUniverse books may be ordered through booksellers or by contacting:

iUniverse LLC
1663 Liberty Drive
Bloomington, IN 47403
www.iuniverse.com
1-800-Authors (1-800-288-4677)

ISBN: 978-1-4917-4845-9 (sc)
ISBN: 978-1-4917-4847-3 (hc)
ISBN: 978-1-4917-4846-6 (e)

Print information available on the last page.

iUniverse rev. date: 4/30/2015

Dedicated to
Andrew, Ayla and Maureene,
Sister Sue
&
Don Isbell for saving my life!

Contents

Introduction

Thirty years after my father's death, I resolved the issues that had haunted me since childhood. Finally, at the age of fifty, the rejection I felt from my father's distant persona was released from my spirit through a conversation with him through the use of a psychic medium.

Through the medium, my father and I talked as adults and were able to discuss some childhood issues about our life together. Many years of psychotherapy and counseling had not been able to make a difference in these father/daughter conflicts, yet five minutes connecting via a psychic medium had performed this miracle for me. I continued these sessions for many years and the book is a summary of those diverse experiences with family, friends and pets on the other side.

My father acknowledged his own shortcomings about his lack of family commitment, inability to demonstrate love, and apologized for not being the father that I needed. My father had remained distant with his two daughters because of his inability to move beyond his own lack of fatherly love during his childhood. I would never have known about his past life if I had not reconnected with him after his death.

I had not initially explained any details to the medium as to why I wanted to contact my father. Yet, somehow she found him in that vast universe and the conversation immediately went to the heart of what I needed to hear. This other side reading (or session) with my father was further validated when my father showed the medium a photo of when I was a toddler. The photo was an old 1952 black-and-white backyard scene with him holding my hand and me staring up at him in admiration. The photo was one of my most treasured memories of us together, and somehow, this photo was sent to the psychic's mind to confirm this connection.

Of course, I had many questions as a researcher and nurse who witnessed death quite often. How does this actually happen? How can I connect to a deceased being through a medium? It is an energy pattern that is left after death from the deceased individual that then becomes quantum particles and accessible to a medium? Are there wave particles or patterns of our former self then encoded on some type of DNA quantum particle that connects to a medium's brain wave patterns in their consciousness during a reading? What is it about the medium's brain that makes her able to connect to the deceased being's consciousness?

My life was changed by that singular moment in time. I hope this book will provide you with some insights and help guide you in your decision to communicate with the other side.

Foreword

This book will share my growing-up life cycles, experiences as a registered nurse, the first connections made with an animal communicator as well as discuss how these prior life journeys contributed to my desire to be connected to the other side. The twenty case studies I have shared in this book are from psychic sessions with family members, friends, pets and even a few people I was not asking to connect with who were deceased. Having had a near-death experience (NDE) after a tragic car accident, in which I did see myself getting CPR in the emergency room, I was motivated to learn more about the Other Side. Like many who have had a (NDE) or Out of Body Experience (OBE), we have turned a page in time with our consciousness that somehow transforms us forever. I chose to pursue Other Side connections due to the one out-of-body experience I had, which eventually lead me to find a way to speak to my father who had died so suddenly many years ago.

After that first Other Side connection with my father, I was motivated to pursue connecting with other friends and family members who had passed away. I had never intended to continue to speak repeatedly to the deceased after the first session, but my interest to contact others just evolved. In the end, I had made thirty contacts with deceased pets and people through the use of psychic mediums. Hence, this book is here to share with you how those sessions impacted my life and that of other people who knew me. Many family members and friends chose to connect with a pet or person through my sharing of these experiences with a psychic medium. These individuals also benefited from the connections and experiences I had with the Other Side. I am hoping you may have a similar experience if you choose to do so as well after reading this book.

Why read this book?

I do hope you can gain insight about life after death from the lessons I learned while connecting with the Other Side. My intent with this book is to bring some understanding to those who question life after death from a somewhat non-religious basis. For those of you who continue to grieve about the loss of a loved one, I hope this book will provide some support in knowing what transpired during my connections with the deceased. There are some continuity in themes throughout these twenty sessions that helped me believe there is some consistency in what transpires on the other side.

I am still not sure why my journey took this path. However, I feel destined to share it with those of you who take the time to read this book. When I reach the Other Side, I too will learn my own life lessons about my earth-time existence of negatives and positives. I already know which negative exchanges will be brought before me during that review process, which is often referred to as the judgment day. From what I have witnessed from my connections with the deceased spirit, is that we must acknowledge those "transgressions" from our time here on this planet. After a review of one's life when on the other side, the spirit seems to work toward a further understanding of his or her life choices. It seems that the deceased spirit confronts those weaknesses and grows in consciousness when they experience this aspect of life after death. Whether that next journey is then experienced through another life form or, they remain in a "heavenly place" for eternity, I do not know the answer. I have the impression from the two sessions with my own father that spirits can remain accessible to the medium long after a death. I can only assume he remained in an Other Side place since he eventually greeted my mother at her passing 40 years later. I was able to confirm their connection after her death with the Psychic Twins, Linda and Terry Jamison. They had shared with me that my parents were together when I made contact with the Other Side three weeks after my Mother had died. It was an incredible relief to me to know they had reconnected after so many long years apart.

In summary, I am only sharing what I have learned in connecting with deceased spirits and acknowledge this is only my opinion. Having witnessed some other psychic TV shows, where mediums do connect with the deceased, it seems a bit inconsistent with what I shared in this book. It is by no means a complete or comprehensive understanding of all that occurs after death, but the book does explore a dimension of existence after death through conversations with the Other Side.

Disclaimer:

I am not writing this book to test out the religious or ethical beliefs surrounding this topic of the afterlife or other side. I want to share this journey as it happened to me. I believe people who read this will understand more about reputable mediums and why I decided to reach out to contact loved ones who have died. I learned from other souls in the afterlife about the continuum of one's spirit after death, as well as how to live now in the present with a more kind approach to the people I share this universe with on a daily basis. I also was fortunate to resolve some guilt issues with past relationships with my deceased loved ones, both human and animal alike, through these psychic sessions.

My one point to clarify upfront is that not all Other Side sessions have totally positive outcomes. These communications can be intense or even a bit uncomfortable at times. There are still some upset spirits on the Other Side working out their own issues. You may be the one person on this side the spirit may have to deal with in some constructive manner. What I have observed through these Other Side sessions is based on my own personal journey; your experience may be vastly different. What I have witnessed in my psychic communications may not be representative of someone else's or the TV show experience.

As you will read, my experiences with Other Side souls is a much more in-depth conversation and does not just address a few brief issues. I don't know why or how this has happened for me, but I certainly feel privileged to have experienced these sessions with family, friends and pets from a vastly different side of this universe.

Book Outline

The first few chapters of the book set the stage for how I evolved as a sensitive child through adulthood up to my present age, sixty. It provides a back story and a possible foundation for my later in life pursuit of psychic connections with the deceased. I also share a few stories about pet communication experiences since these other side connections provided a comfort level with psychic communication prior to actual contact with deceased human spirits. The pet psychic communications helped me to trust what is transmitted from the other side and the use of a psychic medium. It was only through this trusting relationship with the pet psychic that I eventually felt comfortable moving on to an afterlife conversation with human beings. From my own out of body experience after the car accident, where I had viewed myself from the left upper side of the room as CPR was taking place, I was then totally aware of a consciousness that is separate from my body. I can't say where or how I existed in that moment but my mind was certainly not in my body, but in a dimension watching my body from above. Fortunately, the ER team brought me back to life and I went on to have three beautiful children. Maybe that out of body experience had already set in motion a pre-destination with writing this book. These range of experiences, combined with my past history of death and dying, brought me to the point of seeking out a psychic (twenty-five years ago), well before it was a popular topic in mainstream TV and society.

I have used two approaches to my conversation and connections to the Other Side: one is coined the Back Story and the other Reflections. The Back Story section of each chapter provides a brief history of the person in my life who I connected with prior to their death. The Reflections section is a place for additional thoughts or clarification about the psychic reading. I hope these early chapter sections will help to clarify how and why I chose to write this book. All these experiences are true and in some cases, I have hidden the exact identity of the person involved in the story out of respect for privacy.

W will be the initial used to protect the identity of one psychic communicator since I cannot remember her exact words and do not want to misrepresent any messages. I used quotes when I can recall my own precise words when connected to a reading. The Psychic Twins, Linda and Terry Jamison, are comfortable with my documenting our exchanges and giving them credit for their work. They have reviewed what I have written as well for accuracy.

I am not an expert on Heaven, After Life or Other Side connections. I am just a person who met the most professional and sensitive of psychic mediums who helped me connect with Other Side human and pet spirits. These connections with deceased souls helped to guide, counsel, and teach me about my life so I could grow in my own spiritual search for self. Through these connections with the psychics and other side spirits, I have learned that I am an Empath, was an Indigo child and now am an Indigo adult. I also gained insight into how my own extra sensory perceptions are clearly defined by the term clairsentient and medical intuitive.

I hope my message will assist you in deciding on whether to pursue a psychic medium for your personal interests or when you feel the need to communicate with a deceased family, pet or friend. I found comfort, gained insight and knowledge about the Other Side through these exchanges. I am certain you will have a similar and profound experience with using an authentic psychic medium. I am now passing on these lessons learned from the consultations with the Other Side through the use of a psychic medium to you. I hope that my journey and experiences documented through this book will be beneficial to all who read it.

Prologue

There are some background experiences and traumas from my early years that may have contributed to my inner drive to pursue these Other Side communications. I share these as part of my significant history to provide some insight into my personal struggles throughout my life. I realize now that these communication sessions with the other beings were not originally intended to be therapeutic. Yet, they have helped me in many ways to cope with the loss of family members, pets, past traumas and my own fear of death. Sharing the unusual experiences from my childhood, nursing years and everyday existence lay a foundation for how I evolved later in life. For the one person reading this book who may just be ready to make a connection to the Other Side, I hope these sessions help you with a decision. I can't predict how your connections will turn out, but I am certain you will benefit in some way. I have psychiatrist friend who encouraged me to write this book stating that the anguish and sorrow his patients feel after a death of a loved one often is so unbearable, that the individual cannot move on and function in their daily life existence. I hope for those of you who are devastated by the grief associated with the loss of a loved human or pet, that this book helps you somehow cope with your personal tragedy.

Profound gratitude to **W** the psychic communicator/medium, whose patience and guidance helped me experience these Other Side sessions. Additional thanks to the Psychic Twins, Terry and Linda, who I worked with at age sixty after my mother died and with some personal family concerns over the past two years. A thank you goes to all who read this book, for taking the time from your precious lives to learn what you may with a possible cross-over communication. Profound gratitude is extended in particular to Jan Reeps, a new animal communicator who came to me during the writing of this book. A last and unusual thank you goes to Clint Eastwood for the movie he directed regarding Other Side connections entitled, Hereafter. After watching that film ten times, I found the courage to pursue the writing of this book. Thank you, Mr. Eastwood.

I have defined a few terms that are used in the book.

Clairsentience: *Clairsentience is more than just intuition; it's the ability to pick up on the energy and emotions that surround us every day and from the people they interact with on all levels Someone who is clairsentient feels the energy with accuracy and manages this level of "information". (Well-being.com, 2011)*

Empath: *An empath has the ability to scan another's psyche for thoughts and feelings; past, present, and future life occurrences may be part of what they can scan. Many empaths are unaware of how this actually works, and have long accepted that they were* sensitive *to others. (About.com)*

Indigo: *The word used to describe Indigos includes honest, aware, highly intuitive, psychic, independent, fearless, strong-willed, and sensitive. Indigos are old souls who know who they are and where they've come from in a past life journey. These indigo people come as forerunners from prior worlds to change and help mankind transition to a better evolution for the benefit of the universe. Indigo/Crystal phenomenon is the next step in our evolution as a human species. (Finding source.com, 2012)*

Medical Intuitive: *A person who has a keen or unusual perceptual sense of what may be medically unbalanced in a animal or human. The medical intuitive may be able to touch or sense from a distance what or where there is a problem related to the individual's health using their intuition. (Caruso, 2014)*

Medium: *An individual held to be a channel of communication between the earthly world and a world of the deceased. A* medium *is said to have* psychic *abilities but not all* psychics *function as* mediums.*(Ask.com)*

Psychic: *A psychic ("of the mind, mental") is a person who claims to have an ability to* <u>perceive</u> *information hidden from the normal* <u>senses</u> *through* <u>extrasensory perception</u> *(ESP), or who is said by others to have such abilities. (Wikipedia, 2012)*

Pet Communicator: *A pet psychic, animal communicator or pet whisperer is a person who claims to be able to communicate psychically with animals or telepathically with other creatures. Animal communication is simply connecting energetically to an animal living or deceased. (Karen Anderson blog/website 2012*)

Near Death Experience *A person perceives events that seem to be impossible, unusual or supernatural as a* <u>sensation</u> *or* <u>vision</u>, *as part of the afterlife, reported by a person who has come close to death. Near Death Experiences often happen to people who have been clinically dead or in other ways been close to death, whereby the term "near death experience. (Near Death.org, 2012)*

Other Side (After Life*) A possible reference to heaven, other dimensions or an after human/animal/life environment that exists in a different world than an earth born setting. (Caruso, B, 2014)*

Chapter I

My Back Story: Childhood, Traumas, Suicide Watch and Catholicism

This chapter is written to lay a foundation of how my childhood sensitivities may have contributed to how I perceived the world. I believe my upbringing and past experiences may be connected to my strong desire to seek Other Side communications. I am unsure precisely whether I was *clairsentient* at birth as well as an *empath*, but consider both of these terms as I describe my own growth and development from infancy through adulthood. My skills as a *medical intuitive* did not evolve until I had entered nursing school and worked through up into the level of a Reiki II healer.

The Crib Experience: Early Days

I had just learned to pull myself up to stand by holding on to the crib bars. My crib sat next to my parent's bed, yet I always felt anxious, alone and afraid. One afternoon I awoke from a nap to realize I was totally alone. I can't explain why this memory has stuck with me other than that I possibly became aware, for the first time, I was a separate being from my mother and father. Since no one was with me in the room nor could I hear close by, it must have been a memory of fear and anxiety. The bedroom was a semi-darkened room with a few small streaks of sunlight peering through the blinds as dust mites were flurrying about to amuse me. Somehow I knew my mother was right outside of that window in our back yard. I needed to get her attention, so I did what I did best at ten months, started to cry and cry. Crying became my mantra which eventually resulted in my pet name, *The Cry Baby*. My mother immediately came to my rescue, which unfortunately set me up for a disaster when I reached age four, which you will read about later.

I somehow did not feel comfortable, even as a child, with most of what the world was showing me. Maybe my clairsentience had kicked in so I was sensing everyone's emotions very early in my life. This was very overwhelming to me. I can recall feeling intense sadness and anger in people, even as a very, very young child. My crying made all the family members, even ones who did not see me frequently, intolerant of being in the same room with me. My Aunt Francis was a single woman all her life and never had any children, so to her, I was just a crying "scroochamens" (Italian for pain in the ass) She would say, quite frequently:

"Barbara you were just one big pain in the ass and a cry baby."

I believe my father was not very tolerant of my needy behaviors and kept his distance as well. This anxious behavior on my part laid the foundation for a hands-off relationship with my father from my early years of infancy. My sister, who was two years older than me, had been a much more placid child as the first baby. My father, in particular, felt closer to sister Sue since she had been a good baby compared to my anxiety-ridden screams at the same age. Ironically, my sister was very much endowed with the Italian genes in the family and her dark hair and olive complexion made her a clone of my dad.

I had inherited the recessive Irish genes so I was blue eyed, blonde ringlet curls and had pale white skin.

My parents were both brown-eyed, brown-haired dominant so my father would often say to my mother, "Flo, I know you didn't have any other men in your life before me, but how the hell did we end up with a child with blue eyes and pure, white blonde hair?"

In the early 1950's not too much was known about recessive genes but my mother gallantly defended my lineage, stating, "my own dad had been blue eyed and blonde haired as a young child, so it must be his genes."

This theme of being an outsider also raised questions in my mind with grave concerns that I was adopted. Even at age ten, I was still hearing the same questions about my identity and jokes were always of the kind that hurt me. Was she the mailman's baby? One day I packed a small, round red ballet bag and ran away from home for a few hours to sort it all out. I came home six hours later and no one had even been aware I had run away. I felt like an idiot but also realized no one missed me.

My childhood was not a negative experience, except with Aunt D (which will be shared later). Being such a sensitive child, I had reactions that no one understood, not even Dr. Spock had a chapter on me. I seemed to have taken in all those feelings and emotions of others so intensely that I suffered much more than the average child. The latest research on "indigo children" as empaths states that "Empaths" are born into these sensitivities (Indigo Adults, 2011) (1). Many times the Empaths' childhood is often less secure due to their lack of fully understanding why they feel what other people feel so intensely.

The Cry Baby

Having cried more than most babies my age, the pediatrician suggested to my mother that I be hospitalized to determine the cause of my "pain". Three days of hospitalization with the advanced medical health model of 1950's resulted in a very rare diagnosis. The pediatrician reluctantly informed my mother, with great diplomacy and sincerest regrets the following, that *"...unfortunately, Flo, you have a Cry Baby, that is all."*

My mother learned very quickly that the crying would stop if I was knocked out or drowsy with phenobarb elixir, so it became habitual.

Abused, Abandoned, Assaulted and Admonished

It was not my sister's fault she was intolerant of all the attention I received. Everyone tried to soothe my crying episodes just out of sheer frustration. To my sister, it looked like I was getting attention, but it was not positive reinforcement or a sincere interaction. I would be picked up by people but was then able to feel everyone's anxiety when holding a screaming infant like me and it would just get even worse as I could feel their feelings. My sister did what most siblings in rivalry would do and that was hit me when no one was looking. It is the way of the world of siblings but it was never detrimental to my development.

My father then lost his job in 1955 when I was four years old. For a short period of time I had to be taken care of during the day by mother's sister, Aunt D. My older sister was now in kindergarten and I needed a babysitter. Aunt D, who lived one block up the street, made it convenient for my mother to drop me off for childcare each day since she needed to go to work. Somehow my mother had not recalled how moody Aunt D had been as her own mean older sister when she decided to use her to be my childcare provider. After dropping my sister off at kindergarten class each day, I would be taken up the street to Aunt D's house. She had two children at home, one even my age, so it was perfect, right?

At that time in 1950's psychiatric theories, no one completely understood bi-polar disorders. My aunt was a paranoid schizophrenic and definitely bi-polar. Her three children had suffered some atrocities that I won't go into here, but during my short stay at Aunt D's, I learned that crying was the worse behavior in her delusional mind and was not to be tolerated. My parents had used limited physical punishment as a form of discipline. We were yelled at and corrected, but that was the extent of it. I guess my parents did not fall for the traditional model of regular spanking that was so common during the 1950's. Dr. Spock ruined a number of childhoods as did some nuns, priests and bible quotes about spare the rod or spoil the child. I give my parents a great deal of credit for never-hitting any one of us three kids. Unfortunately, Aunt D made up for the lack of spanking by her behavior when she was asked to help out by babysitting me, the sensitive one.

Aunt D's daily childcare was my first experience being totally separated from my mother and my home, so yes, I did cry every morning. I can still remember the dreaded walk up those stone steps to my aunt's house each and every day. My mother would kindly hand me over to my aunt, kiss me on the cheek and say good bye not realizing I was then at the mercy of Aunt D for the next eight hours. I was crying even before we got close to the doorsteps. A wire hairbrush was Aunt D's weapon of choice and there was no chance of stopping her. I still don't understand why I never told my parents what happened every day, but somehow I felt guilty about crying. I thought I deserved to be beaten. I believe it was not so much that the wire brush hurt me but that the abandonment was so traumatic for me. Being left each day to be beaten was not the worst of it, but

I guess I kept thinking my mother would rescue me like she did that first day I was in my crib crying. Since that never happened, I went through life associating my mother and probably other adults, with that experience. She did not know Aunt D beat me. It was not until my Mother was 80 years old that my sister and I shared with her that Aunt D was very fond of wire hairbrushes. My sister never was beaten, but only had her hair pulled painfully into a pony tail by Aunt D. when my mother had broken her arm. Aunt D aggressively pulled her hair to the point of pain; my sister had that trauma as well to remind her of an aunt who was not mentally stable. Ironically, I had not been aware she had suffered this experience until we started talking to my mother about family history almost fifty years later. I developed a basic mistrust of adults as a child and this experience only added to my already anxious personality and crying behavior as a coping mechanism.

Blissful Days of Kindergarten

Eventually, I went off to kindergarten and my mother had to promise that each day she would wait right outside the entrance of the building for me and not leave until I was dismissed. I was so anxious by then that I did not trust anyone, so I made my mother's life miserable. I could not handle being left alone with any adult by that time. Over time I regained some confidence and my mother was able to leave me and return to her job. I then became the Kindergarten Leader of the Pack and was given the important job of getting the milk cartons for "milk and cookie" story time. My one drawback in this time period was that I had lost two front teeth and could not pronounce some words correctly that began with the letter "S". I was immediately assigned special training with the speech therapist. I needed to learn how to use the S sound without my tongue getting caught in between the wide space created by missing teeth. I don't know too many children who can say S words with two missing front teeth, but again, the 1950's was not a time for medical breakthroughs or research on speech therapy. It was a bit of a humiliating time for me since I was the only one in class who needed speech therapy. I do believe, in the long run, it laid the foundation for my future desire to do public speaking to prove that I was a success.

God, Catholicism and the Nuns

Since my mom was raised Catholic, I transferred to St. Bridget's at age six. My sister was there as well. I then learned about God for the first time from the nuns. Somehow my parents never had us pray by the bed at night or read The Bible to us for those first five years of life (or even after we went to Catholic school). So, it was a bit of a shock to go to Catholic School after a year in the free spirited public school system of milk and cookies. There was definitely no milk and cookie time at the Catholic school but the children became pushers of candy, rosaries, The Catholic Times newspaper and even chances for a big win of prayers for life!! Our school had Mardi Gras nights with gambling and spin the wheel for the kids to "play bet." Our parents placed real bets which was used to raise money for the church in those days. I am certain my early years of pushing sales for God's funds turned me against any chance of becoming involved in a marketing or sales as a career .

In school, God was often depicted as a vengeful spirit during the 1950's Catholic Baltimore Catechism teachings. I was never reassured by his presence in my life but only scared more by nuns who beat my knuckles with a ruler just because I would not "control" my vocal contributions during class. I use to get so excited about answering questions in class that I would open my mouth and speak, but was reprimanded for my enthusiasm. My first report card had all A's in my subject matter but a "C" in self-control. I guess I could not be tamed very easily. Fortunately, my second grade experience was a positive one with a lay teacher. Ms. Theresa was great and we had actual fun learning in her class. The public school teachers had accepted my extroverted personality and actually supported me by giving me leadership roles at an early age. Catholic school just repressed my enthusiasm for learning, life and pure joy. Then the day came that was needed to learn about the reporting of daily sins and confession in order to be with God in Heaven. Otherwise, the burning fires of hell would get me. I really became scared and cried an awful lot about the burning fires of hell, as I lay alone in my bed at night. I had nightmares constantly and was just an anxious child. Eventually, I adjusted by being the best Catholic kid on the block; well, close anyway. I just kept praying, going to extra church services, joined the choir, worked as a volunteer for the church and tried to conform, all to avoid the burning fires of hell. My concept of heaven was not a very secure one and certainly death presented itself to a child like me as a horrible end with weird devils waiting to torture me.

I believe the extreme differences in the public school experience and Catholic environment set me up for failure since the nuns did not appreciate my enthusiasm. There were strict lines, prayers, clickers and rulers on the knuckles in Catholic school. I do admit, I loved the Latin word and the Gregorian chant music of the Catholic service. The guitar became their new vehicle of transmitting the word and I became divorced from that beautiful connection by the time high school came around and my hormones were also challenging my faith. Before we leave this childhood of ups and downs, the confessional box deserves mention since it did account for my concerns about monsters, ghosts and burning fire of hell as punishment for sin.

Confession and Catholic Guilt

As a child of 7, I had to make my first confession in order to receive the Sacrament of Communion according to Catholic guidelines. I actually had to make up sins that day for my first confessional box experience because I basically had been so good. I just didn't do the sinful things that had to be confessed like lies or disobedience. I was too worried about the devil and what price I would pay for those sins. So, I decided at age 7 to lie to a priest? At the moment I reached the confessional box, I recalled how the nun pretended she was doing her own confession. She recalled a litany of sins and how to confess, so I stated the same exact sins from our practice session.

"Bless me Father for I have sinned, this is my first confession. I lied four times, had been disobedient to my parents six times and had impure thoughts".

The priest was stunned…"Impure thoughts, " he said a bit too loudly resulting in the nun running over to my little confessional section. Well, my pure mind thought that monster movies were considered impure since they were scary, so I had confessed to impure thoughts. The priest reassured me I had not committed a sin by going to the monster movies, but he could not find a way to explain what an impure thought was to a 7 year old girl. I was so good at being pious that I even spent a summer in the convent at age 12 but boys and hormones certainly changed my direction in life. The nuns also made me clean the floors, wash, iron and do the dishes most of the day. I was not spiritually guided in any way by those chores, so that made a huge difference in why I chose not to be a serious candidate for convent living and the nunnery!

Anyone who was not raised Catholic during the fifties cannot necessarily understand how powerful a strict Catholic school experience was for a sensitive child like me. Many approaches to teaching children the Catholic way have changed since that era, so I do believe progress has been made. Again, my being such a sensitive child possibly contributed to my reactions to the strict nunnery approach to discipline. I became a devout Catholic as a means to survive in that environment but ended up by age 19 becoming a devout agnostic due to reading Bertrand Russell and other philosophers. The age of my mind expansion began with the sixties drugs, music and other intellectual pursuits that presented a different world view than a one-dimensional Catholic existence.

Chapter II

Death/Suicide Experiences

I am sharing this particular story since I believe it also contributed to my eventual desire to understand the Other Side. You do not need to experience ANY of what I did in order to work with a psychic medium and connect to the Other Side. I believe these experiences with suicide and death in the family was a partial catalyst for me wanting to pursue making contact with deceased loved ones. I didn't want my family to burn in the fires of hell at all and suicide was considered a very serious mortal sin in the Catholic faith. The suicide attempts in the family, as well as the successful ones, played an integral role in augmenting my desire to learn more about the Other Side. So, bear with me for a page or two so you can gain insight into how a *child experiences death around them when no one ever explained death to them*.

It seems suicide was a theme in my early life and somehow I became scared of death through whatever was assimilated into my psyche. I later found out in a discussion with my mother that I had two uncles, one cousin, two aunts and another relative I had not met, that committed suicide on my mother's side. Then at age 40 my uncle shot himself, and when I was 48 my cousin, who was Aunt D's son, hung himself in a tree close to his own back yard. The only person on my father's side who committed suicide was Aunt Lena. Eight suicides in one family appear to me a bit extreme. Certainly my family lineage had set the tone for death as an alternative to a most difficult life.

Suicide Watch Assignment-Early Childhood Experiences

I was often asked to go and stay with Aunt Lena overnight on weekends. She had just lost her husband at age 50 and she was terribly lonely. She lived one house away from ours, yet she rarely came to our home to visit. She still needed the company especially during the nights. I did not understand how much her sadness was part of major depression due to her husband's death. I knew she lived in a darkened apartment and seemed unhappy.

As a child of six I could pick up a great deal of feelings from the people around me. I could always tell when someone was lying or being deceitful by their body language or tone of voice. Even at a young age, I could figure out these issues and had to keep silent most of the time since calling attention to the lie would only end up hurting me in the end. I did learn to trust my instincts early on and those readings of people's minds, body language and words made me feel more sensitive to the world in general. I discovered a word for this ability, clairsentient. Clairsentience essentially means, I can feel and sense other people's emotions and pain, which I believed until recently, that everyone had the same capacity. As you can imagine, it was a confusing life for me as a child feeling all these other peoples' emotions. I believe that was why I cried so much even as a very young child. I just felt all that sadness and pain of others.

One day my father came home and was upset, really upset. It seems Aunt Lena had committed suicide and my father found her the Sunday morning after I had spent the night at her apartment. I never really understood what happened since I was not informed about the suicide. I think I was only 9 years old and they wanted to protect me. Yet somehow I knew something was very wrong with Aunt Lena's death. It was not until much later in life that my sister told me about the suicide. I can't even recall anyone explaining death to me; one day Aunt Lena was there a block away and the next she was gone. Yet, somehow Aunt Lena knew I needed closure. She is one of the spirits who connected with me some fifty years later without my requesting a connection. Suddenly, during a different session, the psychic stated someone else is here who wants to apologize for her suicide. Aunt Lena stated that she was sorry she had brought that tragedy to the family. I had not requested a connection with Aunt Lena that day, but she had been on my mind as I was writing this book. Yet, as soon as the portal was opened, Aunt Lena took the opportunity to send her thoughts and apologies to me about her suicide. That is how it happens sometimes; out of the blue when the portal is opened, some deceased being needs to connect. They have processed their earthly life and many years later, they share their thoughts or provide words of wisdom. Aunt Lena did not owe me an apology. However, I was grateful she had the chance to do so, fifty years later. Maybe the entire incident occurred so I could include it in this book and share it with all who read it.

Early Realizations: My Grandmother's Death

At age 12, I did not go to the wake of my maternal grandmother because of my extreme fear of witnessing whatever was there to see at a wake. I should have been able to handle it but my mother did not push me to go. Instead the adults went off to the viewing and I was left at the house alone. My grandmother had been living with us for a few months prior to her death in my parent's room. I went into my parent's room to lay on their big bed while they were at the wake. Suddenly I sensed her presence. It was a scary, threatening moment to feel something I did not understand. I thought it was my imagination playing games on my traumatized mind. It could also have been due to my Catholic guilt since I had disappointed everyone by not being at the viewing. My grandmother's spirit was then felt as I lay there in fear and yes, it was her way of saying good bye to me. She had reassured me that her parakeet, which she let out the window on a cold winter's day due to dementia, was also with her now. I had been so upset the parakeet was let out the window months earlier that I guess she felt the need to transmit she was now with the parakeet? I can only go back in my adult mind and try to analyze the experience since I have learned so much more about death and other side communications since 1962.

Chapter III

Nursing Experiences: Just a Few Cases to Mention

The In-Between Years: Before Nursing School

I have deliberately skipped a few years of my life between the age of 18 to 20 since they were mostly years of leaving high school and going out to work. I did not go directly to college since we were so poor it was not an option for me. I also experienced what the psychedelic years had to offer with music and personal growth. Well, that is another book topic and another set of experiences that hopefully will follow when the time is right.

Nursing School Years:

During my first year of nursing school, I met a woman who was in her second year of medical school. We became friends and I later discovered, within one month of knowing her, that she had very strong suicidal tendencies. I lived two blocks from her apartment and was given a set of keys just in case she needed me to stop her. I was again assigned "suicide watch". She promised she would call me if she felt urges to go that route. This brilliant woman eventually had to take off a semester of medical school to get her head on straight. I received many calls over the last three years of her medical school training when she was still struggling with whether to live or die. Unfortunately, it was usually at 3:00 AM when the questions would arise and I often lost sleep from long late night conversations to keep her alive. The medical student finally stabilized with the right psychiatric medication and has gone on to be a brilliant Intensive care medical director at a prestigious medical center. I like to think I did help her make it to the Big Top of Medicine. At a psychic reading after the first draft of this book, I was informed that this medical student had "hastened her life". This meant she finally chose suicide over life. Obviously getting that message was upsetting for me but she wanted it included in this book, so I have added it per her request. I don't question the message just take what is given to me and put it back out there.

Reflections:

I had no suicide watch assignments other than three during my childhood years until I went to nursing school. I was somehow okay with how these suicide watches evolved over time though I do not know the reason nor understand. Maybe it was my closeness to death from those earlier years yet, it did not seem any more out of the ordinary than any child might have had when growing up. But when the opportunity came around for me to do an intervention, I just felt it was the right thing to do. I don't know how many people would accept a suicide watch, especially since I hardly knew this medical student at the time. It set the stage, at least for me, to come closer to a moment in time when someone might die and I could possibly intervene.

ER and CCU Death Moments:

When a gunshot wound to the chest warranted a cracking of the sternum to perform open heart massage, I stood next to the ER physician as he desperately tried to bring the heart beat back of a 13-year-old boy. The medical team fought gallantly with all the technology available to save this young life. Yet, we failed. I stood next to the young boy in the curtained-off emergency room cubicle alone with only a white sheet draped over his body to cover the cracked-open chest wounds. The family wanted to be with their loved one as soon as they learned he had passed. I was so worried about their seeing any of the major damage we had done to the body in an attempt to try and save his life that I was in a panic mode.

The white sheets we had were not going to be able to cover up the gaping wound in the chest wall or all the blood puddles on the floor of the cubicle. I had the family wait just a few more minutes so I could move some patients around for privacy (at least that is the excuse I gave them.) I spent most of the time making sure the room was presentable for them to visit. I felt this young boy's presence in that room knowing he would not depart until they had their time with him. I did not realize what I was feeling was real. Nursing school had certainly not prepared me for that level of care.

The family came in the cubicle and just then a beautiful warm white glow of after death appeared on this young boy's face. It was like an angelic presence. The mother stated softly, "he is with the Lord now." I was so relieved that I had made some type of contribution in assisting the family with an adjustment to losing their 13-year-old son. It was so tragic and yet, it was a reflection of the horrors inner city black youths must face each day to survive in their world of drugs and violence. This event occurred in 1985 and yet, we are still seeing today how these tragic deaths for young black males seems to continue to challenge how society can best take care of this cultural conflict.

The Unhappy Rooftop Jumper:

One night I was assigned to the Emergency Room and an ambulance arrived with a man who had "jumped" from a rooftop. He was approximately 25 and his flat affect stunned me into a painful connection I was not sure I was experiencing. His arm had been almost torn off and all that remained was some exposed skin and bone. Waiting notification that the surgeon was ready in the Operating Room, this guy needed non-stop monitoring and a suicide watch. He was still conscious enough to get up and out of bed even with a great deal of morphine in his system for pain. I was surprised he was that alert. No one wanted to be in that room with him, so I stayed and was assigned the case because it was the right thing to do. I felt his pain and agony; I was meant to be there that night at his side.

The totally blank stare and flat affect of this guy had me a bit thrown off guard and confused. I was chosen as a safe guard and watchful companion to him for some reason. The blood pressure cuff was tightly wrapped on his injured arm to stop any further blood loss. I just sat there on a stool and continued to monitor his vital signs. No other staff member could handle this scene or his emotions, yet he never said a word to any of us. I know this was depressing to see such a young person want to take his life, but these are medical professionals who could not handle it. Yet, they could handle gunshot wounds, major trauma and other psychiatric challenges, yet here I was again alone doing suicide watch.

The rooftop jumper never spoke a word to me during the hour I sat monitoring his blood pressure and heart rate. I would look into his eyes and he would just stare back attempting to tell his story to me through some other type of communication. I have never witnessed someone as depressed as this guy was that night. I don't know why he jumped off the roof, it may have been to get away from someone chasing him or a burglary, but he would not speak at all. As the

Operating Room (OR) staff arrived to take him to repair his arm, he slightly turned his head to acknowledge me on the way out of the room. Just a glance, then eye contact and he said, "thank you, blue eyes." Wow, the most powerful thank you I ever had in my entire life as an RN. I know now, as I realized then, I was touching him with my feelings of acceptance and care; no words needed, just feelings.

California Dreaming:

When living in California, I became friends with a physician who I worked with only once a week. As luck or karma would have it, for the entire five years I was employed at this job, the physician asked me to keep suicide watch over him. I worked with him professionally so it was a bit weird to know his inner issues; yet, he took great care of his patients. I must have seemed like the type of person one could trust with this task, but again, why? He too promised he would call me if he had gotten close to that point of seriously taking his own life, so we could process his emotions. Fortunately, I had no close calls with him as well but spent a great deal of time in conversations due to his extreme depression. I certainly would have reported him if I felt he at all had jeopardized his patient care, but that was not the case. I moved away and never heard either way whether he continued on with his life or chose to hasten it through suicide.

One Woman who pleaded for Death in the ICU:

A sixty-five year old woman had been in the ICU for over three months with heart failure. She was repeatedly brought back from the brink of death over ten times through CPR and other interventions available in our 1976 technology. Her family did not want her to be signed off as "do not resuscitate." She could not speak due to being on a respirator, yet she was able to fight tooth and nail so we would not suction out her fluids. She was about ninety pounds and strong enough to pull our hands away. She kept shaking her head, "no, no". As nurses and doctors, we all knew and understood she wanted to die but her family members wanted her to stay alive. She suffered many ICU psychosis episodes, a condition brought on by lack of sleep and constant interruptions when a patient does not get restive sleep. None of the RN's wanted to be assigned to her since we all felt so bad that she was being "forced" to stay alive.

Ironically four months after her admittance to the CCU, she finally left in a wheelchair for home. Her family was elated and felt they had done the right thing by her keeping her alive all those months. She then died a week later at home by taking an overdose of pills left by her bedside. It was her desire and will to die. She had to have known what the Other Side was like from the multiple times she existed in a near-death state. I understood these experiences as a young nurse but again, somehow sensed there was more to the feelings. Who would not want to go to the Other Side once they had the experience of bliss and the light? Maybe that is why, according to psychiatry research, the chance of someone committing suicide a second time and being successful, is at a moderately high percentage rate because that closeness to death is not a threatening thought to them.

Reflection:

I became involved with communicating with the Other Side for personal reasons later in life. Yet professionally, I seemed to have accepted death as a RN differently than my peers. Colleagues and patients alike sought me out for my ability to deal with the intensity surrounding the hard cases. I had a healing career for life that started at birth and evolved into a death healing of sorts through my nursing career. There had to be a reason I pursued communication with the Other Side so deliberately. Seriously, who wants to actually be communicating with deceased loved ones on a regular basis? I believe my father's early death, along with unresolved issues, was the main catalyst for my desire to connect to the Other Side. I was fortunate to have crossed paths with **W**, although I believe that fate played a major role in my having met her through an animal-communication workshop.

I do understand the services John Edwards provide are crucial to the emotional well being of others. It is a gift that has helped many as evidenced in the books written and regular sessions on TV. I just don't know how I evolved into pursuing this type of communication years before those people became famous, other than wanting to make peace with my own fears or concerns that had left matters unsettled when someone had died. I am not a medium, but an intensely feeling and sensitive person that just yesterday had a weird experience with a dog at an Vet Hospital. So, I will share it here since it was s suicide request in a manner of speaking.

Suicide Watch for a Dog? Pleading for Death

I had taken my cat to a veterinarian who does advanced trauma and medical care just two days before my final editing of this book. My cat had fallen off a wall and needed surgery and a metal plate put in his leg to hold his bones together. As I was in the waiting room, a woman came out of a clinic room door holding a huge Doberman Pincher on a leash. He was massive and one could see he had been a champion. His demeanor was depressed and with his head down he appeared to me as somewhat unhappy and not interested in his walk outside. He had bandages around his body and a blood catching pouch stitched onto the right side of his body near his kidney. I was immediately drawn to his pain and looked into his sad eyes from a distance. The dog then aggressively pulled his master over toward me and just stood looking into my eyes and soul, so close to me, so

21

intensely. I don't know if he realized I had felt his pain or not, but all I kept hearing from him "please tell them I had enough." I was shocked, was I really hearing this or just feeling it myself? I could not have told his owner since the lady was there with her young child who obviously worshipped this dog. Did I do the right thing in not saying a word?

It was an intense experience I did not know how to handle, so I did nothing except to try and balance the impact of my words with the human need to hold on. I knew from past experiences, which you will read in the pet communication section, that pets are very loyal to us and stay around much longer due to that devotion. They endure a great deal of pain to keep us strong until they are ready to let go. Once they get to the Other Side, they are instantly relieved of their pain and young again now ready to romp and play in what is often called The Rainbow Bridge.

The Academic Suicide Lady:

I had just graduated from nursing school and took a special training to work in the Cardiology Care Unit (CCU). I just loved cardiology and was thrilled to be chosen for the advanced training in that department. I had handled emergency situations quite well during my nursing school years, so I was equipped to handle heart attacks and major medical disorders. One day I walked into the CCU and my supervisor wanted to speak to me immediately. I had been off duty that weekend and was getting an update on my patients. She shared that a suicide case had been assigned the only bed left in the hospital, a CCU bed. So, the woman was in the CCU until another bed in the psychiatric ward was available. It was the norm anyway to keep a suicide attempt in an ICU for 24 hours just in case there were complications, but this was my first experience when working in this particular CCU.

This suicide lady had thrown out every nurse who came into her room who tried to take care of her over the weekend. The supervisor did not know my past history of all those suicide experiences in the family, yet somehow she sensed I could handle this case.

I went into the woman's room and just sat quietly next to her bed. She did not ask me to leave. I just sat there and accepted her silence. She looked into my eyes, and I communicated acceptance to her as best I could, and then after a full hour, she began sharing her story as tears rolled down her cheeks. She was a vice president of a college in another state and she did not share all of what had happened. She felt she let many people down somehow and chose suicide as a solution. It is a hard reality for someone to wake up after attempting to commit suicide and it does <u>not</u> work. One can imagine the conversation with oneself "Oh _____ I can't even do suicide right"!

This professional lady was dealing with all those feelings of failure, on top of her personal issues, and now she added a failed suicide attempt. She was embarrassed, humiliated, and her anger was reflected in how she treated the nurses. Somehow we connected. I took care of her for the rest of the week until she was transferred to a psychiatric facility. Whatever innate gifts I had developed over the years of just listening, and being accepting of an individual's life choices, seems to elicit the sharing of many intense emotions.

Given these experiences were between the years 1951 and 1984, essentially infancy through young adulthood, Other Side communications were not acceptable or hot topics for society to discuss. Even when living in laid back Southern California, the land of innovation and extreme movements in societal norms, I never heard any physicians or everyday people discuss Other Side issues. Possibly I was not running with the innovative psychic groups to be aware of how this topic was addressed in 1980, but eventually I caught up with the research on this topic through a personal experience.

Chapter IV

Early Beginnings:
Animal Communication:
The Baby Steps

My communication sessions with the Other Side relatives occurred almost thirty years after my father's death. But my communications started about 15 years before my first experience with him through the use of this pet psychic. At a pet store one day, I noticed a flyer advertising "animal communicator will speak about making connections with your pets". I signed up for the weekend course and met **W,** a woman who was an animal communications specialist. At that time I had 3 dogs, 8 cats, 4 gerbils, 4 tree frogs and 3 horses. With three children, a stepson and tons of animals in the house, and in school for my Ph.D., I needed all the help I could get with the pets. I took the course for my own well being and interest in psychic relationships with pets and to help my husband deal with his frustration about too many pets for one household.

I also needed some type of insight into how to keep these pets manageable and healthy. My husband was not pleased I had this little farm and was very angry I spent so much money on pets. I was particularly motivated in using animal communications to be certain these pets behaved so I was not in conflict with my husband about their care, inconvenience or costs. I also was particularly motivated to learn to communicate with my German shepherd dog, Ursa, who was my soul mate in this life. Please note this animal communicator training was booked in 1986 when NO ONE advertised for this type of service nor did many believe it was even possible. It was almost a hidden society of believers and it certainly was not as popular and accepted topic as it is today. I knew that the feelings I had in understanding patients might be tapped into for animals, so I was excited to learn if I could help my own pets and learn how to manage what was a bit overwhelming to all that visited our home.

At this first Animal Communication workshop day, I volunteered to be the test person to have a spontaneous reading in front of the entire group. The other 10 participants sat there waiting for **W** to demonstrate her skills about animal communication through me. I had hoped my dog,Ursa, who was twenty miles away, would make contact and tell me how he felt. Our pets were not permitted at these sessions, but somehow **W** instantly was communicating with my horse, Badger, and not with Ursa, my dog. Badger told the communicator that I needed to learn how to sit better in the saddle, handle his bridle and gear more skillfully, and that I should take riding lessons. I was so stunned and embarrassed at that moment but the horse was so RIGHT!! I could have easily said that it was not my horse she was talking to and reiterate I had excellent equestrian skills, but I could not say it was not I. The truth was so astounding to hear from the horse's mouth, which I replied, yep…he is right. I need more riding lessons and softer skills when handling equestrian equipment and the horse.

At that point, I became a dedicated believer of psychic communications. My horse was miles away and the animal communicator was making a connection with an animal I had not even mentioned to her in any descriptive way. Yet, she went on to describe his markings and color perfectly. I was hooked and fortunately, my children loved the idea.

My husband was willing to try anything to cut back on expenses and the commotion associated with a household of critters interfacing with humans. Two of my three children now continue to use **W** to help them with their pets, so they too have learned the advantage of having this type of communication with animals. I have also passed her name and services on to over 100 people in the past twenty years, all are quite satisfied with her abilities.

Household Pets: Twenty Years of Help:

Rose Dust: The Run-Away Cat

My first cat as a married woman with two children was Rosie or RoseDust. An independent and confident feline, Rosie was named after Grandmom Rose, my paternal grandmother. Before we had her spayed, she went into heat at five months of age. Having run away to find her mates, we were devastated when she could not be located. I called **W** and she stated, "Rosie is hiding under a car not too far away". The kids and I walked around the cars close to our home and found Rosie, mating with a black male tomcat directly across the street under the car of our neighbor. **W** was right; Rosie had been gone three days and had fortunately stayed close to home. Unfortunately, we had no idea how close to home she was until after we spoke with **W**. Rosie had mated and had five beautiful kittens, so it was an amazing experience for the entire family. The only black kitten was immediately adopted by my son Andrew. It was his very first pet and lived with him for seventeen years. The black kitty was named T.C. for a friend named Terry Connor, who died of AIDS.

Rosie went on to live for nineteen years, advising me to accept things as they are through my animal communicator. I continued to speak with Rosie over the years after her demise just because she had such wisdom to share. Rosie had never been sick a day in her life (other than having run away one time). It seems Rosie was trying to calm my restless and anxious spirit and have me learn to be mellow as she had been.

Rosie made one last stand as an independent kitty by returning to our old home after we moved four blocks away to accommodate our growing family. I went every day to look for Rosie and **W** kept saying she was right in the old neighborhood. By the time I made it back up the street after speaking with **W**, Rosie would take off from that spot because the new homeowners kept chasing her away. An entire month had passed and I was certain Rosie was still there at the old house but worried she was sick. **W** confirmed Rosie was still alive but barely. **W** said, "Rosie is under a bush near the old house".

I immediately drove to the old neighborhood to find Rosie in the yard across the street where she had been mating with the black tomcat 10 years earlier. She was weak, dehydrated, and had worms and diarrhea from eating out of trash cans for thirty days; she was almost dead. I rushed her to the vet and she was hospitalized for three days on IV's and antibiotics. Rosie came home to the new house never to roam again. Then, 19 years later she died in my farm home with no assistance from a vet; because that is the way she wanted it, her way. I buried her right in the backyard area and visited her gravesite frequently. Rosie told **W** in a reading I had requested a day before she died that her "mommy" would let her die the way she wanted to, in her own time. She died with my dog Ursa, having helped her pass an hour after I had left for work that day. When I came home for lunch three hours later, Ursa was sitting in the bathroom having stayed with Rosie after her demise. Ironically, in turn, when it was Ursa's time, another kitty named Little Puffer would stay with him through his own sudden death in the same exact spot, in that same exact downstairs bathroom. Rose communicated with me after her death and continued to tell me I needed to calm down, which unfortunately, took another ten years to do.

Squirty: The Rejected Puppy

Squirty was born the runt of the only litter from my male German shepherd, Ursa, when he was six years of age. Ursa was my soul mate and an incredible dog, so I was hoping for a clone of him from the mating. I had purchased Aspen, the female, from a breeder in Massachusetts and Aspen was shipped to Philadelphia. The morning of Aspens' delivery was a freezing cold winter's day. After seven pups were born, one last little squirt pup just came plopping out when Aspen stood up to nurse her other seven pups. Aspen smelled the runt and did not groom him. She then picked him up in her mouth and placed him in a cold corner of the room far away from her warm whelping box and blankets. I was stunned. I picked up Squirty, properly named for his size, and placed him back in the warm whelping box. Aspen again picked the runt up and placed him in the same cold corner of the room. I got up and picked up this runt and brought him back to the whelping box with Aspen. I then placed Squirty on Aspen's nipple so he could suckle and he seemed to have a difficult time. I stayed there and informed Aspen she was not rejecting him just because he was the runt. The next day I called the animal communicator so I could speak to Aspen about this unacceptable behavior I was witnessing. Why was she rejecting Squirty as her pup? I needed to know right away so I could fix it and called the pet psychic.

W said, "Oh. … I see, "and could see, via telepathic visualization into Squirty's brain. Aspen told **W** something was wrong with the pup and she was not going to nurse it. **W** stated, "his brain is not wired right somehow, Barbara, I don't know exactly what is wrong, but that is why Aspen is rejecting him." Aspen then told **W**, "well if she (meaning me) wants him alive, she is going to have to take care of him because I won't do it."

Aspen and I came to a compromise through **W**, I knew Squirty needed Aspen's milk for all kinds of reasons, as well as the bonding aspect. I then convinced Aspen to nurse the pup and I was willing to do the rest. Of course, I had to bribe Aspen with chicken the entire time Squirty was nursing, but it worked out. Ironically, Squirty was a male and the only puppy that looked exactly like my Ursa. So after all the pups were sold, it was apparent that Squirty would stay with me. Over time Squirty developed some weird habits like going in circles and bumping into objects. **W** confirmed he was blind in one eye and half-blind in the other and that he had some other seizure issues. Granted, this communication was all over the phone and she had never even touched the puppy.

I ended up taking Squirty to the University of Pennsylvania Vet School's Neurology department after he had a major seizure from his rabies shot. The vets there videotaped his circle behavior and did an MRI/EEG. The diagnosis made by **W** on his second day of life was that, "Squirty had only half a brain and the rest of his brain was not wired right." This is exactly as **W** had told me months before this diagnosis, and now, Squirty also had fluid on his brain. Squirty was placed on Phenobarb since the vets could not do surgery on him to repair a half-developed brain. Again, this was after the animal communicator had informed me Squirty was so sick and had abnormal brain development. After eight months of watching this pup suffer with seizures that were not controlled, I knew I had to let him be euthanized. Squirty would yell in the middle of the night in a sound sleep as his seizures would come on. I would run down to the living room to find him totally asleep from the Phenobarb but still having a seizure and feeling the pain in his head. Squirty told **W** that his head hurt a great deal, so I knew he could not have survived much longer. Was Aspen right in rejecting him? Although I gave him a good quality of life for eight months, I don't know if I did the right thing.

The neurology department at Penn was startled when I explained that an animal communicator informed me that Squirty had something abnormal in the wiring with his brain. Not that they thought it impossible that there would be a brain disorder, but that an animal communicator was the one who had accurately diagnosed it. I did not have the courage to share with the Penn vets that **W** had performed this diagnosis over the phone, telepathically.

One week later Squirty was dropped off at Penn for an MRI and EEG to evaluate his brain status. The neurologist called me at home and was a bit humbled by the findings. Dr. Maroon stated that Squirty did indeed have something missing in his brain development; he actually had only one side of a brain that evolved to a full capacity. The rest was just some miscellaneous nerve cells. Squirty was definitely ¾ blind and he also had a fluid filled tumor on the base of his skull. Somehow Aspen knew these deformities were serious enough that she did not want to keep Squirty alive. I, on the other hand, wanted to do all I could to keep him alive; unfortunately that would not be the case. Aspen was right from the start, Squirty should have not been permitted to stay on this earth in the condition he was; unfortunately he had suffered. Phenobarbital did little to decrease the seizure activity. He was obedient, walked on a leash and was non-aggressive even with just half a brain, although deathly afraid of other dogs since he could not see.

I finally conceded when Squirty was eight months old. I drove home from Penn after Squirty was euthanized, crying my eyes out. I decided to call **W** to make sure Squirty had made it to the light. Squirty had yet another surprise waiting for me; a last minute of new insight about the Other Side that I could not have ever imagined nor had the animal communicator ever experienced it in her time of doing this type of work. **W** connected to the puppy telepathically and started to speak to Squirty, which at that point she stated,

"That is strange. He is lying on your kitchen floor; well his spirit is anyway." **W** stated that *"Squirty has not gone to the light since there certainly are no kitchens in the afterlife. He is in your kitchen now!!"*

I was stunned and so taken back that this poor creature was still here in my presence. **W** even felt into his head pain and said,

"Oh gosh, he is so confused about what has happened that he doesn't know to go to the light."

I immediately had **W** contact my other dog, Misty, who had passed over three months prior due to stroke. **W** located her on the Other Side and asked Misty to lead Squirty through the light to the Other Side. Misty was not at all happy about the assignment given she had just left this puppy who, while on earth, was a big pain in the butt to her because of his many complex behaviors. Misty reluctantly agreed to urge Squirty to go to the light and he then communicated through **W**,

"Are you sure I have to leave my mommy"?

It was such a heartbreaker knowing he was willing to stay in this in-between space and spirit form just to remain faithful to me. **W** felt Squirty's pain in his head because he had not passed over and was still here on this earth. Not all dogs go to heaven, or at least not right away, until they are encouraged or lead by another good dog and a great psychic medium. I am certain these circumstances are rare and happen when the pet is not prepared to cross over. I actually had one similar experience when a five-year-old dog with a heart condition had to be euthanized. She actually rode home in the car with me after being euthanized, according to **W**, since she did not understand what had happened with her sudden death. I am ever haunted by the pets getting confused and whatever role I played in that confusion. This was a lesson well learned.

In the end, **W** convinced Squirty to go to the light where he could be pain free, play, and be able to see the world with his full eyes. The moment Squirty crossed over, **W** said he was running, playing and finally seeing all the beauty the afterlife had for pets at The Rainbow Bridge. I was so happy for him. And there Squirty will wait, now with my Ursa, to greet me when I crossover. Thanks again to **W**, I was at ease with this final decision and knew Squirty was safe and happy in the afterlife.

T.C.: The Black Cat Who Loved my Son:

T.C. was the only black cat in Rosie's litter. As stated prior, my son Andrew picked out the black one and named it after a friend of mine who died of AIDS. T.C. was special from the start; loving and very devoted to my son. When my son finally had his own apartment and was working. T.C. went to live with him. They had seventeen wonderful years together and **W** would help us again to let T.C. pass to the other side but ONLY when my son was ready.

At 17, T.C. had become very thin, had not eaten and my son found it so hard to say good-bye to his very own kitty. It was time to let T.C. go. Witnessing my son having to euthanize T.C. was almost unbearable for me as a parent because I felt his emotions as well as my own. A parent having to watch their child, no matter what age, euthanize their pet is a paralyzing experience where no amount of empathy seems to help. When animals breathe that last sigh of relief and their spirit is released out of the diseased body, it is a most difficult moment even when knowing they will feel no more pain. Yet I was quite disturbed because T.C .had cried out in pain when the vet kept trying to find a vein to send the medication into his system. T.C. was so dehydrated that his veins had collapsed. Hearing the cat cry only made my heart ache so much more and it was not at all a good experience for my son to witness.

About a week later after T.C. had been euthanized, I asked **W** to confirm that T.C. had gone to the light. I needed to connect with

T.C. because I was so upset he felt pain his last five minutes of life. That experience had never happened before when I had to euthanize a pet. To have this instance occur with my son, was just way, way too upsetting to me. When I reached T.C. through **W,** he was so wise and gracious in his understanding of my emotions surrounding that moment of pain. I apologized to T.C. for having to experience any pain at the end, blaming myself for the vet's lack of judgment. T.C. said,

"It was a fraction of a second in the realm of time and existence here, please do not burden yourself with these thoughts".

Here a cat was sharing his wisdom with me from the Other Side, so that the next time I went through a similar experience, I would not torture myself emotionally. And on top of it, I learned that there is a continuum of time and existence that will extend beyond that moment of death. The wisdom of what T.C. shared in one sentence impacted me deeply then and forever in my time on this earth now.

Reflection: A year after T.C. was euthanized Andrew was ready to talk to him again. **W** found T.C.'s spirit in Andrew's bedroom and T.C. stated,

"I come and visit my boy from the light sometimes to watch over him".

I learned another lesson about the Other Side through this connection. Our animals can come back to visit and still be with us in a special way. I never would have known about the possibility without this Other Side communication with the pets after their death. I hope in some way it helps those of you who have lost pets to know they are still around you and visit to lie at your feet or just be in your presence. So for those of you who have "thought" you felt that presence, you were not just imagining it; your pet had been there to spend time with you!

Butterscotch-The Orange Kitty

Butterscotch was a kitten we adopted from a barn cat mom, and he was just a love bug. Somehow he gained a great deal of weight and was the "fat cat" out of our eight family cats. Unfortunately, we actually then began calling him Fat Cat. It seemed that the other cats picked on him and we did not know why. After contacting **W,** it became apparent that the other cats in the house made fun of him because of his weight. Wow, can you imagine realizing that the cats have these emotions and can be communicating it to each other? That is not at all what I expected to hear from the animal communicator when we checked in with Butterscotch in a reading one day. Placing animal actions and emotions into a human category is not what some scientists believe can even happen.

Butterscotch had run away from home due to the constant teasing by the other cat members of the house. He was gone for four days and we were all devastated. Ursa, my dog, tried telling me Butterscotch was under our shed by going to the backyard area repeatedly when we asked him to find the cat. We checked and could not see or hear our kitty at all. Ursa kept going to the shed door and we would open it, removing every item in there and there was no Butterscotch anywhere. **W** then said the cat is stuck way underneath the bottom part where the dirt is and wooden beams line the base of the shed. Again, this was done all by phone.

We then took our flashlights outside at night and placed them exactly where Ursa kept standing by the shed side door. Behold an orange kitty eyes stared back. Poor Butterscotch had somehow become stuck, due to his larger size, in the space between the dirt and boards holding the shed up, exactly as **W** had said. Our neighbor retrieved his chain saw and we cut open a large hole to lift Butterscotch out of his prison. Five days without food or water and, yes, Butterscotch had lost some weight. You have to ask yourself, was it intentional on

Butterscotch's part? Five days of Ursa going to the same place to tell us he found the cat, yet we could not figure it out. Only **W** and her hard work with Ursa gave us the reason to look one more time in our back yard. Ursa said later through the animal communicator that:

"I kept showing them the spot where the kitty was but they never looked under the shed, just inside".

Wow, we were ignorant humans. Before I leave the pet section of this book I do have to mention two other unusual pets that were reached by a pet communicator.

Ursa Boy: My Soul Mate:

As mentioned previously, this unbelievable long-haired German shepherd puppy was my very own first dog that was all my responsibility. Ursa picked me out when I went to see the breeder. I don't care what everyone says, that was the best way for me to know he wanted me. When all the other ten German Shepherd puppies were bored with me and ran off to play, Ursa sat on my lap and stayed. It was a sign for me that he wanted to be my dog.

There are many stories about Ursa, but one sticks out the most. When I was living alone after being divorced, Ursa kept waking me up in the middle of the night for some reason. I did not know why, but as it turned out, I later learned that I had sleep apnea and he was waking me up when I would stop breathing. After I lost 40 pounds the sleep apnea stopped, so all was okay. Yet, one other night, two years later, Ursa woke me up again. I knew I did not have sleep apnea but watched Ursa as he went down the stairs from my bedroom at one in the morning. I finally got up thinking Ursa had to go outside to the grass area to relieve himself. When I got up to let him out the side door, it was open. I thought that I had left it opened and Ursa was waking me to alert me to close it. The next morning at 6 a.m I received a call from my credit card company asking if I was missing my credit card. They informed me that someone had used it at various stores and gas stations throughout the night. I immediately went to where my purse had been by the side door where Ursa had led me during the night. The money holder with the credit card was gone.

I then called **W** so she could speak to Ursa. Ursa had heard the burglars when they were in the house and tried to waken me up. When I did not wake up and did not move, he again went downstairs and pinned the guys up against the wall. Then to protect me, Ursa told **W** he ran back to the bedroom and woke me again. **W** was able to get a description of the two guys from my dog. I did not have to pay for the $5,000 credit card splurge, and I realized the burglars were former workers who had done repairs in my house. Ursa had tried to let me know about the burglars but only through the animal communicator was I able to piece together the entire series of events. The police officer was able to accept the story about my dog since he had heard of psychics helping to solve cases from other area officers. Eventually, a woman was videotaped in a pharmacy trying to use my credit card and caught. I was fortunate to have my animal communicator assist me with this problem and a detective that believed in psychics.

An Unexpected Death: Ursaboy

Ursa died at age 10. One day he did not eat his food and I knew something was wrong. I intended to take him to the veterinarian the next day, since he rarely passed up a meal. Ursa stayed outside until 9:00 PM that night and did not want to come in. I eventually urged him into the house and fell asleep on the couch watching TV. I thought Ursa might have to go outside again in the middle of the night so I stayed on the couch for ready access to the back door. At 1 a.m. in the morning I was awakened by a loud meowing, like a female cat in heat. My gray kitty was crying and crying so loudly, that I thought the cat was stuck in a closet. I eventually found the kitty lying next to Ursa in the bathroom, the same bathroom he had stayed in when Rosie had died. Ursa had died and now Puffer, another kitty, was calling me to let me know he was gone. Ursa was still warm to the touch. I can't go into any other details about my extreme sorrow over his loss but the animal communicator did check in with Ursa on the Other Side for me that very same day. Ursa said:

"I just felt dizzy and then a horrible pain in my head suddenly happened. I was then looking at a bright light with all the cats and dogs I knew from our home were waiting for me at the light".

Ursa became a puppy again once he crossed over, and was able to play with his family pets that had died prior. I will never get over that loss but knowing Ursa will be waiting there for me helps me deal with the immense loss and the missing of him on a daily basis.

Lou, The Iguana

I had adopted an iguana from a disabled friend and it was a totally new experience for me. I guess somehow I did not think **W** could talk to an iguana as my assumption was it was only dogs, cats and horses. **W** often communicated with my iguana who then helped me understand his needs. Lou was very emphatic with what he wanted and I became actually closer to this pet since I felt I had a connection with him. Lou was able to tell me that he needed more warmth and liked certain foods more than others. When I needed to move to a different home, Lou was quite old. He asked politely if he could be let loose to experience the real world before he died. Fortunately, through the animal communicator, I was able to let Lou go and he ran up a tree and lived his life for the last few days he had left, in the wild. What a beautiful way to let him go.

The Scorpion Show Down

Now, one last pet experience, well not really a pet, but a creature experience that will blow you away since it is not the norm but way outside the scatter gram of life. I had moved to Arizona and lived in a house with a few acres of land. **W** was kind enough to fly out with my daughter with all eight cats. Yes, all eight were flown from Philadelphia to Phoenix. Once **W** arrived at the house, I had shared with her that I was deathly afraid of the scorpions that lived in the back yard. I had a few in the house as well and after growing up an East coast girl, scorpions posed a real threat to my mental sanity. **W** told me that she could ask them to stay out of the house and just remain outside. I was stunned. You mean you can talk to scorpions too? She then politely explained to the scorpions in my back yard that I would like that they stay outside my home, out of respect. The scorpions actually responded with:

They are building something over in our usual home area and we are being given less space to live out here in the desert, so we moved close to this house since no one was actually living in this house for so long.

As it turned out, a new building was going up about a mile from my own backyard where a school was located. The scorpions had migrated to my area due to the bulldozer tearing up their regular home site. What could I say? Well, I did state that I preferred for them to not come into the house but to live out in my yard and not sting the cats or people that lived there. Through **W** we came to an agreement so that all creatures and humans could live peacefully. Can you actually believe that negotiations were taking place between a group of scorpions and myself?

Saving and Finding of a Lost Kitty: A new animal communicator experience

Sophia a 17 year old indoor condo cat escaped to the wilderness one week after I moved into a new home. This Sophia came to me via my son who had moved too and could not take his kitty due to his girlfriend's allergy to cats. Sophia was set in her ways, loved indoor life but did enjoy her outside city roof view. She told the animal communicator, when my son called to tell her she would be moving in with me, that she did not like other kitties. When my son said, "you never lived with other kitties"! Sophia responded, "well I just know I won't".

Sophia's strength and an animal communicator' gifts saved this cat from a tragic death by a fox or some car accident. Sophia did not know the outdoors and had escaped the day before I left for my new job training in Ohio. I was hysterical and to boot, I had to be able to learn new computer technology and new documentation of electronic records files when I was under this worrisome state of mind. I had my sister post flyers and she was called once about the cat markings and was at my home every day, no Sophia.

When I returned five days later from the Ohio training, I went door to door for the first ½ mile circumference of my house and spoke directly to people. The last couple I met had been visiting a friend and did not live that close by. However, they kindly took the flyer with them in case they knew someone else who saw the cat.

By Sunday I was frantic, so I picked up the phone list of animal communicators and needed to find one who would work with me as an emergency and was on the east coast time schedule. I went to the page of animal communicators in the Pennsylvania area and one photo stood out and as kind, calm and gentle woman who was holding a horse's bridle and had a warmth that I could feel across the pages of time. I viscerally felt she was the right one to call. I left a message at 8:45 AM and she called me back by 9:00 AM. I was very fortunate to have found her and trusted my gut to lead me to the right psychic. Jan immediately took in all the information and said she would call me back after she tried to locate Sophia. Approximately one hour later, Jan called and did find Sophia who was alive but very weak, tired, dehydrated and disoriented/confused. Having never ventured outdoors, Sophia was definitely lost and could not even find her way back to the house.

Jan described the yard and the back white pillar porch, so off I was in search of such demographics. I stayed within a ½ mile of my home never thinking Sophia, who also had arthritis and was overweight, would make it too much further away. I searched the yard near by and could not find the white pillared porch and just kept calling Jan repeatedly to see if Sophia could hear me. Jan was so patient and tolerant of my frantic calls and said Sophia was definitely at the house nearby that had white pillars holding up a backyard overhead roof that was an outside back porch. The vegetation near the back porch was tall palm tree bushes as described by Sophia showing that to Jan. Fortunately, the next day I received a call from the lady I gave the last flyer to and she said, "I think your cat is in our backyard eating our cats food". I rushed over and discovered it was more than a mile between the two houses, so I had not looked that far the day before. To my joy, Sophia sat on the back porch with two white pillars and overhead roof cover top. As I lifted Sophia into my arms, I was so grateful for the skills of an animal communicator Jan. I cried tears of joy and relief knowing I did not have to tell my son the sad news that I lost his cat.

To have to have told my son that his 17 year old cat is lost or possibly dead was unbearable for me as a parent to inflict that kind of sadness and be the responsible party. Jan did a great job and without her help Sophia might be gone forever or still wondering about with people feeding her off their back porches. Sophia would never had made it out in the cold winter weather storms and she would not have survived the fox, a car accident or even other feral cats. However, her life was spared and I am so grateful for Jan's help. I sit here typing up this added story to the last section and watch through my bay window as Sophia walks outside in freedom. She stays in her own yard after commanded to never leave the property again through the animal communicator. Sophia has listened well and has been obedient, she loves her outdoor life now and comes in and sleeps with me. Yet without Jan's help, she would not be here to enjoy her first fall season and the feel of leaves under her paws nor the touch of a wet snowflake upon her nose, if she had passed. Thank you Jan for helping save a precious kitty cat's life.

A second lost cat and Jan again came to the rescue?

My three year old Bengal Ender has suffered the faults of being a throwback. His genetics did not do the job of setting him up to be domesticated even those he was a seventh generation split from the first desert Asian Bengal. By the time the Bengal is sold to the public, they should be calm and ready for indoors life. Ender suffered greatly by being kept captive behind windows that showed him his real world of existence. Ender escaped twice only to have been hit by a car, which punctured him a lung as well as blew out his shoulder. Six thousand dollars later and Ender was healthy and had no limp, although the vet told me for sure he would walk with a great impairment. Ender beat the odds. Then again a second escape and somehow he must have fallen from a tall tree, since he was not used to climbing them. I found him two days later limping back to me a mile from our home as I called his name into the woods, he barely could walk. Yet with his back left leg held high, Ender ran to me as his savior. Again he had a punctured lung, a crushed nose and a spiral double fracture on his left rear leg. Again, the same surgeon did a

41

magnificent job and yet again, he beat the odds with no disability or limp, as predicted by the same vet. When Ender returned both times for his check-ups, the vet was astonished by his healing. I did inform the vet that Reiki had been done on Ender for the first four weeks of his injury and that I believe helped him be healed more efficiently and effectively than just lying in a crate for four weeks. I also started early ambulation and helped him regain his strength and stamina long before his six weeks were up.

Ender continued to need to be outdoors, so I caved in and knew his destiny was out of my hands. One too many days he was gone three/four days, and Jan asked him to come home and he would, reluctantly, but he would demonstrate to me he was still alive. Our new house offered miles and miles of open country, woods, fields with mice and plenty of food, so Ender was in his earthly heaven.

One episode was unusual when he did not return for a week and Jan found him somewhat groggy and confused. Ender felt he was in someone's back enclosed screened in porch and appeared to be upset and anxious. Ender refused to tell Jan whether he was hurt, yet she picked up him being groggy but not in pain. Ender then went quiet and would not talk to Jan. Jan was worried he was being despondent but said he definitely did not cross over or pass away.

A neighbor had seen one of the posters I had put up to try and locate him while Jan still believed he was in a house. This new neighbor meant well when she showed the poster of Ender to her friend who was also an animal communicator. She did not ask my permission but, I know in her heart she was trying to help. Ironically, two days later she came to my house to tell me that Ender had passed away due to dog having killed him. She stated her friend told her Ender wanted me to know so I could move on and not keep worrying about him. The message was that he was now at the Rainbow Bridge and to please keep my heart open for another kitty in the future, do not be so saddened by his loss.

Jam totally disagreed and said he did not pass nor have a traumatic death. She kept saying that animal communication is not an exact science but in her heart, she felt he was still here and not deceased. I spent that night with no sleep trying to see what my other cats were telling me. I knew Jan had said they were upset by Ender's long absence, but they were mourning his not being at the house. Yet I began to feel like they were mourning his death and spent the next full day at work in total belief that yes, my Ender kitty has now crossed over and the dog had killed him. I just felt I could not torture myself any further and although I trusted Jan, she had not been able to get Ender to talk to her for a few days and she was worried too. Jan was certain he was still alive and I had to trust her instincts rather than the other animal communicator who I did not know about or have any prior experience with as stable and accurate information.

I came home early that day from work out of sheer inability to think clearly. As I arrived at my doors step, I heard a cat cry and behind me was Ender saying I am here and I am alive, but I am not trusting of you or any other human. He looked scared but was definitely not hurt, a little thinner but just was afraid to go into the house. I finally left the door open and Ender came in to eat looking up as if I was going to snatch him or hurt him. I then closed the door behind me and Ender spent about an hour in the house and got restless right away. He did allow me to pet him and since he was due to a flee treatment, I put that on him as well. Ender just had a look in his eye of fear and I did not want to make him fear me or my entrapment of him. So, I opened the door. My rationale was that Ender would then know he could come home and be let our again. I wanted Ender to trust me that I would not lock him up again and again, since that appears to be what had happened to him with whoever had stolen him.

Ender did return the next day to eat and visit, and again I closed the door for a brief hour of time and let Ender out again. He was even less happy this second time around and now has not returned again after three days. I spoke to my vet who believes he needs Prozac to calm him down. Jan did a few readings on Ender once he was home and he still won't talk about what happened. It is almost as if he has post-traumatic stress disorder from being locked up somewhere against his will. Ender will not open up to Jan right now, but knowing Jan has such a good heart, Ender will eventually find solstice in searching out Jan to tell her his story. I also have asked Jan to check in with Ender's brother Sparkie since often Sparkie knows what has happened to Ender and will tell us the truth if he knows it. One time Ender had been stuck up a tree for three days due to some fox chasing him and did not come down for a long time due to being in fear for his life. That time Ender was gone for five days and finally returned but he was not the one who told Jan what had happened to him, it was Sparkie who shared Ender's story. Ender was too humiliated to tell Jan the story himself including the part where once he got down from the tree, he happened to turn the wrong way which added an additional day to his travels back to me. Ender has a very strong independent stoic spirit and does not want anyone to know he had failed or faltered and comes across as if he was a macho man too manly to have made such a simple mistakes.

So at this writing, I still have no idea what happened to Ender out there on the road and in the house he was caught in. Hopefully, Sparkie will give us an update when Jan speaks to him in the next week.

Sophia's Choice

Sophia did not choose her life partners yet, she was a cat who accepted her lot in life with some resistance. As an animal cannot communicate their wishes nor plan out their destiny, Sophia lived a condo life for seventeen and half years. Sophia did what all indoor cats do with boredom, annoyed her owner my son with her little obsessive compulsive needs. Crying at the door, asking for food incessantly and wanting water from the bathroom sink, were just a few of her particular habits. Her last two years of life she had significant change moving from an apartment to a condo with an outdoor roof. Now Sophia had a new door to meow at and could actually go out and enjoy a rooftop life with a full view of the Philadelphia skyline. Just as she settled in, her life was now asking for yet another change in the form of a major move to a home with three cats and a dog.

As my son was moving to Boston with a forever partner and she was allergic to cats so Sophia could not go with him. Sophia with all her baggage and a tumor in her belly had two choices: euthanasia at age 17 or come live with her son's Mother who had three other young Bengal cats and a dog who protected his kitties fiercely. I chose life for Sophia and requested that she have a chance to live at my 15 acre home so she could see and feel what her instincts were all about and enjoy her last few months.

She still hissed occasionally and reached out a paw to the other cats, but mutual respect endured. One of my fondest memories of Sophia is that she would walk with me each night as I did my check of the property rounds as part of an exercise routine. I would make a large circle around the borders of my property with a parade of animals following behind me. Sophia would insist on leading the pack and had to be the first one behind me as the dominant leader now. She outranked all the boy cats and as the elder, she deserved respect. Sophia had lost about 3 lbs which is a lot for a cat and she was now in good shape, could walk for thirty minutes, chase a ball and actually run after a squirrel or bird. Sophia's instincts were in full form. She would only stay outdoors for about a half hour tiring easily now at age 17. Her jumping up on the rocks each night for her special affection time, we would sit and take in the stars or sunset. It is a beautiful moment in time etched forever in my mind. She would sit peacefully amongst the other three cats and dog as our pride regrouped each night in a way to bond and share love as a family. It was a ritual that gave me so much joy since it seemed that no matter where my other cats were in the world, they somehow would end up and do our parade each night to gather together to share our family time at Ender's Rock. Ender had been killed by a car ten days earlier, a tragedy that could not be avoided given his lifestyle. Fortunately Jan had helped me through the shock of it and gave me peace of mind knowing he did not suffer and he was in the afterlife.

Sophia was well aware of Ender's death and my crying made it apparent of how the impact of my personal guilt affected me. Trying to keep all kitties indoors was difficult but I had trusted Sophia to keep her promise and after three months of never roaming off the property, I believed she would not break that bond. My human mind was not prepared for Sophia's final choice but it was a lesson learned like no other about animals and animal communicators.

The day Sophia got out was literally a mistake since I was to leave on a business trip and had all the kitties inside. I was getting ready to pack up my luggage when I noticed her missing. The cellar door was left ajar by our dog walker who did not realize it needed a complete push to shut, so now, one hour before my departure on a trip, Sophia was gone. She had not left the property for three months so where on earth was she? I panicked having just lost Ender ten days prior. I thought," no I can't take another death this soon", and yet, my heart told me something was very much wrong. Sophia was now nowhere on the property and that was so uncharacteristic of her undeniable obedience to the rule of never leaving the property lines or go in the street.

I immediately called Jan my animal communicator and she said, "Sophia is up high, like on a shed or tree and is afraid to come down, but she is very bewildered and confused". So I canceled my business trip due to the stress I was feeling plus I was very sick with a bad upper respiratory virus and could not drive the four hour trip.

I walked the neighborhood calling for Sophia and the animal communicator said she could hear me, so I knew she was in walking distance. I roamed the area near the house when finally my Munchkin cat Wiggie, who had escaped with her, showed up walking down the road with a look on his face that told me something was terribly wrong. He followed me home and came in the door with no coaxing or resistance which was not his usual demeanor. He was communicating something I did not want to acknowledge, Sophia was gone. I immediately called Jan, the animal communicator but she was in a meeting, so I got in my car. I drove a half of a mile to find Sophia's beautiful little body in the middle of the road where her brother Ender had died as well, crushed by a car and dead. I stopped all school buses and traffic as I picked up her still warm body and put her in my car with a covered mat. I was devastated and so angry at the universe for giving me a second blow. I screamed out and cried and asked why, why did she leave the property? She knew what I needed for her to be safe. The answer would come later that night when Jan returned my call to tell me the following:

"Sophia knew her time was done her on earth and her tumor was becoming a painful process for her. She knew you had plans to have vet care for her in the end. Sophia did not want to go that route nor did she want you to go through that with her for your sake. Sophia had finally known what it was like to be an outdoor kitty and using her instincts, wanted to use those instincts one last time and decide when to die. Sophia wanted to choose death on her own terms and chose to go to the spot Ender was killed to hasten her own death. In essence Sophia committed assisted suicide as most animals in the wild do when it is there time. Lioness walk away from their pride to spare them the pain of seeing a pride member die. Sophia took her own life to spare me the pain of the long months of slow death that I had endured with so many of my other kitties these past twenty years. It is hard to see our pets go downhill, lose their dignity and then euthanize them all for our sake so that they stay with us when we need to let them go.

Sophia's Choice was that she would take her own life. I was also informed with great relief that animals are literally taken out of their body prior to the last moment of death and do not experience pain. They are not experiencing what we see as the end result of a car accident. Jan has told me a few times that the universe takes care of animal and literally extracts their spirit/soul out so they don't experience a traumatic death or the painful process. I was relieved to know Sophia did not experience that pain, but still my heart ached. According to Jan, Ender was there on the other side to greet Sophia and have her come to him as a family member who, although they had not been best buddies on this side of the earth, they are now soul mates in the spirit world. I will see them both again when my time comes to cross over.

Can we accept as humans that animal have the ability to think through and plan out suicide? Not really, but they do know when their time has come. I have to respect their wishes. Sophia only knew that Ender had died on a road not too far from home. Sophia had no other reason to leave this home and had not done so in three months. That does not relieve me of my guilt in any of this nor do I accept I was not ultimately responsible in the end for any of my pets' tragic death. It is a hard line to walk once I opened the door and started to use a animal communicator to connect. Once I knew how our pets think and feel, I could not deny them their requests to use their instincts and be outdoors. I pay the price with grief, sorrow and unending guilt. Yet, now my other remaining two cats have reluctantly accepted that staying in will make me not scream and cry again, nor cause their death. They have agreed, only out of respect for my wishes, to stay indoors against all that their instincts drive them to do. Cats are not like dogs and once they do take in the beauty of nature and those instincts are stimulated, it is so hard to turn it off.

Sophia taught me so much about aging and finding joy even in her last months of life. The last night Sophia showed me so many pieces of herself that only in retrospect did I see it as a last good-bye memory to me. At 7 PM Sophia sat next to me by the computer and once she saw a squirrel outside, took off like a kitten to chase the squirrel up the tree. I laughed so hard as she was just so happy to be able to do that as an instinctual behavior. She then was seen playing with the dog out in the grass; she had never chased him nor played tag and she was rumbling in the grass with the dog. I again was in awe of her new found joy in life. One last joyful gift was that she came and slept with me her last night on this earth, having cuddled up next to me. She finally was part of a family who loved her, enjoyed her short time with us and will be missed so much even only after four months of her sharing this life with us.

Sophia's Choice is one I still am struggling with as I tears fall from my eyes in writing this story I have chosen to share with you. Please remember your pets have emotions and feelings that we have yet to understand. Their instincts are there each day and yet they chose to live and die with us as guardians and beings of such beauty and spirit that we are so very fortunate to have them love us. Thank you Sophia for choosing me, thank you for loving me.

Grief resolution happened, through the use of the animal communicator Jan, was the only way I was able to get through this ordeal. I would have blamed myself for years over Sophia's death if Jan had not told me that Sophia chose to go to the road to die knowing that is how Ender had been killed. She stated to Jan she knew it was her time and she heard Ender calling her to come to the other side. I realize that is a hard story to accept but I do believe that is what transpired. I am fortunate to have Jan help me resolve the guilt and know that Sophia was in the afterlife free to roam and play as a new kitten again. One snowy winter's day I walked the grounds and felt Sophia's presence beside me. Sophia let me know she is happy in the afterlife when I spoke to Jan later that day.

Summary

This summarizes the examples of my communications through a pet medium with animals both alive and deceased. So as a family, we all felt blessed to have **W**, and now Jan, in our lives and their gifts of communicating with our pets both while on this earth and in the afterlife. Both of these animal communicators presented their information similarly yet reached out to the pets in a different set of ways. Jan liked an ongoing dialogue with the pets as a way to communicate and **W** did one time interventions. Yet having worked with them over the years, I had developed a connection that was acceptable to all parties involved.

Reflections:

So, after twenty years of successful communications with my pets I was most comfortable with using a psychic medium. I began sending friends with pets to **W** and they as well had a great experience. However, **W** had never told me she could also channel to deceased people due to her need to maintain some privacy in her own life. Yet, one day the topic came up as I was mentioning my father's death at a young age and how it impacted me. **W** then shared that she can also talk to humans on the Other Side as well.

Chapter V

The Lessons Learned from Family Members and Friends

The First Contact Ever – My Father - 30 Years After His Death

I had struggled for 50 years feeling rejection from my father's inability to demonstrate love even before he died which continued on after his death. During the 1950's era, fathers were often the breadwinners and out of the house frequently. My father's lack of attention and distance may not have been perceived from the outside as neglect or abuse, but emotionally, I was devastated. My sister, after reading this book, reflected that she thought my father had a low level of chronic depression. We were very poor; we were often seen searching in the couch cushions for a quarter to buy a carton of milk on Friday mornings. Payday was always Friday, so those mornings we were definitely depleted of funds.

My father worked as a laborer cleaning bathrooms for our local city wide playgrounds. He mopped floors, did outside landscaping, mowing and preparing the fields for sports events using lye to line the marks for the playing fields. After years of inhaling lye and smoking a pack of non-filtered cigarettes each day, my father had developed cancer of the lung. By the time he was diagnosed at age 50, it was in an advanced stage. Complete removal of his left lung was necessary. In 1973, removing an entire lung was a very risky procedure and he was not in the best of health at that time from obesity and undiagnosed diabetes.

All of my childhood into my young adult years I felt his rejection was a personal one due to my crying syndrome as a child and sensitive nature. I now believe more of his withdrawal was due to his own chronic depression. As an accomplished musician he also led a very unfulfilled life working in manual laborer. We rented a home my entire life, never owning one like some of our neighbors, so poverty was a result of his inability to provide for his family.

I took all these emotions in and as an empath, felt even more insecure blaming myself for so much of his unhappiness. I could not, as a child, sort out one emotion from another, hence I took it all as rejection. I was only feeling the negatives of his lack of affection and he never wanted to hug, hold or be interested in my life through most of my teen years. I yearned for affection now by any male and none of my family male friends met that need or served as a role model. Eventually, when hormones kicked in at age 13, I soon discovered boys and became a boy crazy girl. I was not sexually promiscuous but craved the affection boys could give and they always wanted more than just a hug and kiss.

My father had no idea how sensitive I was and how I took to heart all that was said and done. My sister read this book and could not believe we even came from the same family or had the same parents. She was in disbelief at the way I had experienced the world with such emotions and sensitivity. She was able to handle more of the detachment of my father because of her different personality type. That was a valuable lesson for me to learn that maybe my parents were not that bad at nurturing as I believed, but due to being an empath, I would say my experiences as a child were still extreme. Why? My dad might make comments to my brother like,

"John, one day we are going to run away from these girls and go to Disneyland and visit California and never come back".

As a child, I really believed that was going to happen, so my fear of abandonment was always reinforced by these comments and actions of my father. My father never read a book to me or put me to bed. It wasn't until I visited other friends houses and had a sleep over did I know that parents read books and put their children to bed. My father did, once, make up a kids bedtime story when my mother was sick with a stomach virus. It was a silly homemade story about a tomato in the woods. I loved it and felt so overwhelmed and attended to that he would actually spend the time telling us a story. We had books as children but there was no nightly ritual of reading, laying in bed and cuddling or even being tucked into the covers. It was part of the reason I think I was so scared of the dark, closets and being alone.

Eventually, my father did see I had some talent when I became an accomplished classical percussionist and he witnessed my skills at The Philadelphia Academy of Music. It was a few proud moments when I know my father enjoyed me for me. My athletic accomplishments and academic success was not really ever acknowledged with any verbal praise or a hug/ kiss. After high school graduation I worked as a lowly clerk typist at the Medical College of Pennsylvania, formerly Women's Medical School, in Philadelphia. It was a short walk from my house and I was trying to save money to move out on my own. Only one month after I had moved out (one block away from home to my own apartment) did my father become seriously ill. One day it was pneumonia and then next day, cancer of the lung. So his death was very sudden and a traumatic experience for me hence, my desire to connect with him on the Other Side.

The Surgery, Death of My Father
and a Afterlife Connection

My father was operated on in 1973 when a total lobectomy, or removal of a lung, was not a well-established surgical procedure. My father was really frightened the day he left home to go to the hospital. He looked at our dachshund dog Rommel, as his last glance back on the way out the front door and said:

"I will never make it back to this house".

It was as if he knew it was his time. He never kissed us kids good-bye but only spoke to the dog, which he adored. I did visit him the day of his surgery and what transpired stays with me to this day. As he was wheeled into the surgery suite, he turned to me and said,

"You will make a good nurse".

Those were his last words to me since after his surgery he was not able to speak due to being on a respirator system for breathing. I had just been accepted to nursing school a week before his surgery, so that was again, a precious moment in time where he actually said something caring to me. Ironically, I am certain my father knew he would not survive the surgery, so it was almost as if he wanted to get a few good words in before he passed. Two days after the surgery, we received a call that my father had taken a turn for the worse and we had to come to his bedside.

The Death of My Dad

At 1:30 a.m. I was called at my new apartment about my dad's sudden decline. My boyfriend, who had ironically stayed for the first time overnight, accompanied me and drove me to the hospital. Just that afternoon in the ICU, my father had greeted me with a playful exchange asking if my West Highland puppy was okay. My puppy had seizures and my Father comically put up his hands on his ears and waved them like a bunny rabbit. My puppy was pure white and small but he had pure pink bunny ears so, he did look like a rabbit. I was so thrilled that afternoon that my father even cared enough to ask about my puppy that it stood out as one of the most precious memories of my father in my entire lifetime with him.

As I entered the hospital ICU room that night, my family was around the bed in solemn vigil. My father was no longer on the respirator but laid peacefully with only a heart monitor hooked up to him. It appears that somehow my mother had made the decision, based on my father's request with his physician's approval, not to be resuscitated again. Since my mother knew that the cancer had spread to my father's heart, it would have been a painful six months of dying at home. My father did not want that type of death, so he had chosen to have all life-saving equipment stopped.

The heart monitor just beeped slowly down to a low alarm which announced the final beat of his heart had just occurred. The RN politely and respectfully came over to the bed and shut off the monitor. We all just stood there in silence. As I cried, my mother tried to usher us out of the ICU room. Again, the cry baby in me just could not hold back at this tender and tragic moment in time. I immediately resisted and went back to my father's bedside. I leaned down to his ear and said, "I love you, Daddy". I realized that was the first time I can ever recall telling my father I loved him. So, having been raised in a family where that was not a spoken sentiment, it was a huge moment for me to say those words. I know now, after thirty years of nursing, that hearing is the last of the five senses to go when in a coma or even a few moments close to death. I guess I intuitively went to his ear and whispered I loved him. I felt good about that final exchange and as karma would have it, those words were again spoken but back to me by my father.

A First Other Side Experience: My Father

When **W** had realized my father had been deceased for thirty years, she said that she may not be able to reach him. **W** stated he may have already moved on to another life. I was not expecting either of those comments, so this was news to me. Eventually, **W** connected with my father after I described only a few features. She found him sitting along the Schuylkill River fishing with my uncle and he turned to acknowledge the connection by saying through **W**,

"Little one, how are you?"

I don't remember exactly how I responded other than saying I missed him. I talked about my Mother's deterioration with dementia and that she needed to go to a nursing facility. I explained she did not want to go into a nursing home and he replied,

"Your mother was always her own person; I had difficulty with my own relationship with her".

He stated he would go into her dreams and try to help her see the benefit of going to a nursing home. I asked him about the rest of the family and he stated, "they are all here." **W** then relayed that my father was sharing another memory with her to authenticate I had really reached him. **W** said to me,

"Your Father is driving a jeep in an army uniform smoking a cigarette."

W herself was confused at first by this image. I then realized it was an old image he was sending to validate to me it was him and that only I would recognize a piece of his past history. Yes, he was in the Army during the war, and yes, he drove a jeep for the Colonel. Unfortunately, he was smoking cigarettes then as well. My father stated that he was proud of my many accomplishments and was sorry he had not been here on this side to share those with me. He also apologized for not having steered my brother in the right direction when it came to the understanding how to be devoted to a family. He admitted that he had

"Not done right by you girls. I just didn't know how to handle you at all; I left that up to your Mother."

My father then said,

"I know I didn't take care of my family and do things a father should have done, for that I am sorry."

W then stated he was somehow now communicating, through images to her that his own father had been a vicious, mean man saying nasty things to him about his neck looking like a chicken and his nose being so big. So, my father's own experience in being loved by his father was far from a good one nor did he have a role model to have witnessed a close, loving family as well. **W** shared that my dad sent her the message that he was raised in the Italian macho style of being a man and it interfered with his ability to be a good father. I was just so overjoyed at the connection that I had very little to say about my own issues. Then **W** stopped very suddenly and stated:

"He is walking away now".

It was as if the time in the portal had been depleted. We had actually spoken for about ten minutes and that was long overdue. **W** said, but wait your father has looked back over his shoulder and said,

"Yes, I do love you."

That was all I needed to hear to heal from the years of rejection and pain, as well as the lack of affection from my father. Those words released my soul and spirit from the long-term pain like no other comment would have accomplished. The fact that my father had to die and cross over to learn he loved me, did not take away from the fact he could not show his love for me when on this side. Somehow it just made it all better for me and within a fraction of a moment in time with the Other Side, I felt loved by my father; finally at age 50.

Not everyone is prepared to hear or confront the past traumas when connecting with the Other Side, but I was fortunate to have a good medium. Counseling over the years helped me be ready to deal with that moment in time and be healed! I believe that there is value in seeking professional help; a psychic medium cannot take the place of a good counselor.

Reflection:

W just reports what she sees or hears, she does not try to interpret it for me. She is a conduit for an exchange of information. Yet, unfortunately, **W** can also feel the pain, anger and sometimes the love being expressed through her by the Other Side connection. I, as you can imagine, was so elated after this exchange that I called all my friends and family to share this joyful moment. From my past history, this exchange with my father was a monumental change from what I had experienced as a child in my connections to him. Not all my family embraced this psychic exchange, and I can accept their skepticism. I do hope this book does convince them there is a benefit to these types of connection.

Chapter VI

The Good, the Bad, and the Ugly Side of Other Side Connections

My ex-boyfriend from California had spent quite a bit of time doing drugs when I first met him. Eventually he was selling marijuana as a means of income and I became very uncomfortable with it all. As an RN, I had a great deal at stake by living in a house where marijuana was stashed in barrels in our ceiling crawl space. It was 1978 and I had moved to Southern California as a way to explore the world and move away from the East Coast memories. I eventually encouraged my boyfriend to move back East to the Boston area, where he grew up, when we discovered his mother had liver cancer. He had been away from home for over ten years and it was time to move away from the drug infested environment he had become so accustomed to in San Diego.

We moved back East and had a good year living in Cohasset, a beautiful coastal town south of Boston. J was still buying pot on a regular basis but there was no dealing. I had a great job and was somewhat happy but knew the relationship with J was not going to be one that would last much longer. J had some great qualities but his brain was not interested in anything academic and between being an electrician and smoking pot every day, J had little to offer me as a future husband.

J's mother passed away just after we had been there a year. J immediately wanted to move back to San Diego. He was not happy away from that Southern California scene. I was very happy in Cohasset, yet felt compelled to stay with him and support him through a most difficult time. J, like me, had a very distant and unaffectionate relationship with his mother, being the only boy and the "baby" he did have a good relationship with his father. J insisted on the move to San Diego and I felt obligated to stay with him during this traumatic time in adjusting to his mother's loss.

Once we moved back to San Diego, we actually rented the same place we had left only 18 months earlier. It was probably not a good omen, but again, I was trying to be as kind and caring because of J's emotional confusion after the death of his mother. He had many unresolved feelings that he did not want to process so I was just his buffer for the adjustment to her death. In the long run, it was good he had spent that last year with her and his father, since I believe he did make some progress with his feelings as a grown man. It is my assumption that he was a person who just had to suppress his emotions through daily drug use and I had little insight into addictions at that time not recognizing how dependent J was on all types of drugs and alcohol. He had managed to conceal it from me fairly well in the two years we were together.

I eventually left J six months after returning to San Diego and lived in a part of town far away from our beach place. I was working as an RN and was getting pretty stimulated by the intellectual environment I was being exposed to at the hospital center. I was encouraged to go back to medical school by one of the doctors I worked for and I had given it serious consideration. Prior to my moving back to

Philadelphia for graduate school, I had dated one other guy about five months after I had left J. This man happened to be of Mexican and Native American descent. I still don't know how it got back to J, but he was so upset I was dating a "wetback". I was not of the same mindset and one of the reasons I could not stay with J was due to an experience I had with him only six months prior. We had a camping adventure as a celebration of our return to San Diego with a few of his friends. We went to Yuma, Arizona to camp along the river and do some boating. A Hispanic family was camping next to us on the Yuma River. The friends and J had been so mean and made derogatory remarks about their being "wetbacks" that this family left in the middle of the night out of sheer fear for their lives. I knew then, at that exact moment on the Yuma River, that I would never stay with J and that my connection to him had been mesmerized by the California Dreaming experience. Now, almost a year later, I was dating this Hispanic man and J had somehow heard through a mutual friend that I was involved in a relationship too.

I was away skiing in Big Sky with my new boyfriend when J had a major car accident. It was quite a life threatening accident and the only reason I was informed was because the Emergency Room contacted me from San Diego. I had placed J on my health insurance policy as my live-in partner when I started my job upon our return to San Diego. I had obviously not taken J off that policy, so I was contacted to be certain I was still willing to have him be treated since I was away on a vacation at that time he had the accident. I, of course, said that he was still on the insurance and we were not officially separated. This plan paid for all of his ICU stay, hospitalization and rehab from this horrific accident.

I had heard through a friend that he was so devastated about my dating a "wetback" that he got drunk one night and was trying to find this man to beat up when he had the accident. Things with J and I had not been in a good place before the accident and now, I was even more sure I had made the right decision in leaving him. I did not, however, go to visit him after this accident due to my anger toward him for his actions. It was not until four years later, that I went to see him when planning to move back East. I had decided to return to Philadelphia to attend graduate school, and felt it was a good time to say farewell and leave on a positive note. I felt obligated to put an end to any animosity between us. My last good-bye was not well received and it was most difficult for me to leave my dog, Cardiff, with J forever.

Well, as life would take its course 34 years later I received a call from his sister, also an RN, who stated J had died from a brain tumor. He finally had married someone from AA and was clean/sober and happy with this woman. Unfortunately, his life was cut short and he died after months of suffering. I did feel quite bad for him and for the way we had left our last connection in San Diego. So, out of guilt, I decided to contact him on the Other Side to make amends.

Do not assume that your guilt can be resolved by speaking with someone on the Other Side in every instance, so be prepared for any session to not go in the direction you had planned. **W** made the connection and immediately there was negative energy being transmitted through that portal opening and it went like this:

J said, *"What do you want and why are you even here?"*

Wow, I was not expecting that reception and **W** did nothing to break it softly to me that his anger was apparent. I told him that I just wanted to say how sorry I was that we had taken the road we did and that learning of his recent death, had motivated me to connect with him. J was not at all pleased to be intersecting with me since I guess that his negative memories of me had not yet been processed. J went on to say,

"You went your way, and I went my way so why are you even connecting?"

I was at a loss at this first-time negative exchange, so I was able to pull a thought out that seemed to calm the situation down for the moment. I asked J,

"What happened to my dog, Cardiff, that I left with you when I moved back to Philadelphia?"

J, in all of his anger directed at me, decided to re-enact the moment of Cardiff's death in living color through **W.** Instead of just stating, Cardiff died after being hit by a car, J chose to hurt me by actually providing a blow-by-blow description of the incident. He described in detail from the moment he found out Cardiff had escaped out of the yard to the moment he picked him up dead off the streets of San Diego and put his lifeless body in the back of his van. The rest of the session only went downhill and there was no learning lessons shared by him and it was apparent he was still working on his issues in whatever dimension he was existing in at the time of our connection.

Reflection:

I was not prepared for this intense and sad exchange and neither was **W.** I told J that I appreciated him taking care of Cardiff after I left San Diego and that again, I was sorry we had parted on such negative terms. To be honest, I can't remember the very last words said other than that **W** was eager to break the connection as much as I was. I learned a valuable lesson about the Other Side; expect the unexpected; don't assume because one connection or two went so well, that the rest will follow suit. I was disturbed by that experience but had hoped that somehow it was all put to rest for J and that he could now move on to a good place on the Other Side. So, I hope that by now, J has moved into a better quality of existence on the Other Side and is happier.

A Troubled Cousin's Suicide

My cousin suffered the trials of his mother, Aunt D, much worse than my daily beatings in the morning drop off battle of wills. Yet, my cousin had successfully managed to have a musical career, was married and raised three children by age 45. All seemed on the surface to be a success to those around him. When Aunt D was alive, she would threaten to commit suicide about once a month calling my mother to come save her from putting her head in the oven. I am certain my cousin DB and two siblings, had it much worse living there during their years of growing up in that house. I know from my own days of experiencing Aunt D, both as a child and adult, my cousins led a tortured existence on many realms even when they had moved away from their mother. DB, my youngest cousin, just walked out to his back yard, placed a rope around a tree and hung himself at age 45. I needed to find out why and really wanted to help his family (wife and three children) understand what happened. They were blaming themselves and were suffering. I called the medium **W** to ask for some help. She was able to locate DB from my description of his hair and facial features. When she located his being, she described that he was wearing a red flannel shirt with black stripes and jeans. No one would know except family members that he died in those clothes. **W** was then suddenly uncomfortable and went onto say the following:

"He is in a room and some people are grilling him and asking him why he did it." **W** *then stated it was very uncomfortable for her since she felt his feelings when she connected.* **W** asked me, "did he commit suicide, I can feel something strangling me?" I said yes, (I had not told her that he had committed suicide at that point, and **W** said

"This is not good being here and witnessing this session. We are not supposed to be exposed to this type of situation."

I asked if she would just let him know that I cared and understood on some level his decision to commit suicide. My cousin merely replied,

"Please tell my family I love them and I am sorry."

That was all he was permitted to say. **W** said she had to break off the session since it appeared we were witnessing and interrupting some type of confrontation for my cousin about his suicide. **W** was so uncomfortable that she lasted only two minutes in that state of mind. I did not have the heart or courage to contact his wife to share the message from him. I knew I could never explain how I even had a message given to me from my cousin since so few people 20 years ago were even aware of Other Side communications. Both **W** and I learned an intense lesson; she is not to interrupt and follow-up on a suicide so close to the incident. For me, it is important to be more upfront with **W** about the reason I am connecting so she does not get caught up in such an emotional state and feels the actual suicide attempt herself. I had not intentionally held back information but thought, as was in the past, the less information she knew the more I felt it was a real connection. I had trusted her skills and underestimated the emotional state it would create and she paid the price of the exhaustion from that exchange.

Reflection:

Eight members of my entire family had successful suicides. Two others had attempted suicide. It seems like a strange family legacy yet, it was one of the strongest motivating forces for me to pursue a connection with the afterlife, God, Heaven and where all went in the afterlife.

My Favorite Cousin's Death

Pigeon was her nickname and she was a jolly person with a round smile all the time and cheerful attitude about life. Pigeon loved animals and was happy living with her same-sex partner, two dachshunds and my grandmother. Pigeon had become quite ill over a six-month period and the medical people had called it a bowel infection when in fact, it was a tumor. Pigeon went downhill pretty fast after that diagnosis and there were no choices but hospice. Her sisters gathered around her day and night to care for her and to help support her partner as well during this time of death.

I went to visit Pigeon a few days before she died. Pigeon was lying on a bed with her three sisters sitting close monitoring her every need. It was so beautiful to see that scene of love and care from a family that had a pretty unhealthy history of yelling and anger. In the end, the love was so present that I knew Pigeon's death would be peaceful.

As I sat on the bed, I held Pigeon's hand. Her eyes remained closed but she was fully alert. I told her: "this is Barbie." Pigeon and my Grandmom Rose were the only ones permitted to call me Barbie. She smiled and squeezed my hand and sighed. I said I was sorry this had happened and as tears filled my eyes, she said, "Please don't worry, I will be okay." She suddenly had some type of spasm from the large tumor pressing on her diaphragm. Her sisters immediately gave her a shot of a muscle relaxer to relieve the spasm and Pigeon quieted down. I told Pigeon that she was my favorite cousin of all and that her kindness towards me had meant so much. Being the sensitive child that I was, Pigeon was very aware of my emotions and always was so kind and caring.

Pigeon and her partner Stoney had brought my grandmother to visit me when I had moved to San Diego. Pigeon and her partner had driven Grandmom Rose all the way out to see me and it was such an honor to share a West Coast sunset for the first time for my 80-year-old Italian grandmother. She had never seen the sun set over an ocean and she was mesmerized. It was such a joy to see her experience this moment and I have Pigeon to thank for that special memory.

I decided to check in with Pigeon about a month after her death. When **W** connected, she found Pigeon reading a stack of books. Pigeon turned and **W** described her perfectly back to me; the smile and alabaster complexion which she kept even at age 55 up until her death. Pigeon then said:

"I have a great deal of work to do now since I never really studied or did my academics when on that side of life." The relatives are all here and still arguing like they use to."

Pigeon had worked in a factory all her life and never worked hard at her school studies. I guess her task now was to find a way to make up for that decision. So, this was another part of the Other Side I was learning about through my contact. The first time, I actually asked if there was any message I could pass on to family or friends. I said,

"Do you want me to give Stoney a message"?

Pigeon had only one message to be delivered to her partner.

"Please tell her I miss holding her hand, and, that I wish we had adopted that little boy."

I knew nothing of that potential adoption but after calling her partner Stoney immediately after the session, it was clear they had actually considered adoption. Being two lesbian women in the 1990's, it looked like the chances had been very slim for them to have been able to succeed in adopting a child. I felt so good knowing I had provided her partner with a message that was a special secret between them. It was a way for Pigeon to validate to her partner that it was really her I was speaking to by mentioning the adoption and holding of hands. Her partner was thrilled and tears of joy were shed and her heart was so full of love by this message. I felt so good in making the connection and in providing some comfort to her partner.

Reflection:

Pigeon did tell me that the "family" was still all there on the other side trying to sort out their differences from this side of their prior life. I was not expecting to hear that there was still a working out of family matters especially since it had been some time since many of them had passed. I am not sure what to take away from this statement, other than each individual leaves this earth needing to learn what has to be understood as part of the Other Side experience. I was somewhat confused by her statements about the family still arguing since I would have thought that after twenty years since their deaths, that all of it was worked through on the Other Side. I don't have an answer at all on this information and why it was still a family matter trying to be resolved at this time in their other side life.

A Mother-in Law: A Typical Not-So-Nice Exchange

Without going into any details about my deceased mother-in-law, other than she did not like me and blamed me for all that was wrong in her son's life, it was not a very positive relationship for over 23 years of my marriage. Yet, I still felt compelled to connect with her after she had passed away because I wanted to apologize for our lack of connection in this life. I was divorced from her son at that time, yet had felt it important to communicate with her for my daughter's sake. My daughter was devastated by the first real close family death in her life. My children knew I was working with the psychic medium and they, after years of having our animals contacted on this side, were accepting of my communications with deceased family members as well. So, I chose to connect with my ex-mother-in –law for my daughter's sake just to let my daughter know things were okay.

Edie, my mother-in-law, immediately acted out her usual behavior of a "faked surprise" when the connection was made through __W__ in the following manner:

__W__ reported that, *"She is mouthing an expression like a big "OH" with her mouth in an "OPEN" OH from being surprised, not only by the connection, but by it being you"!*

According to __W__, Edie was taken aback by the fact that I was the one connecting of all people. Edie was still not in a "good positive place as yet". Catholics call it purgatory, and I don't know what in-between place it is or why __W__ picked up on this aspect of the contact. I guess maybe there is a place where we go soon after passing to be challenged with all the negative things we did while here on earth. Edie's reply at realizing she could make a comment to me through this visit was merely,

"I know I could have been kinder to you".

Well, that was the only acknowledgement Edie had ever made that she had had been a nasty person to me as a daughter-in-law when on this side. __W__ responded by saying, "I don't think she has reached the good part of the other side as yet, it appears she is in some type of limbo place and is working on her legacy of negativity.

The other thought communicated to me from my mother-in-law by __W__ was the following:

"Take good care of my girl, Ayla, and tell her I love her. I didn't get a chance to say good-bye."

That was the entire exchange, there was nothing else that I wanted to say nor did Edie.

Reflection:

My daughter cried when I shared the above comments with her that her Grandmother loved her and wanted me to take good care of "her girl". I know my daughter felt special to have heard that message from her grandmother. I think this session was a more neutral other side exchange. I do feel somewhat relieved that Edie acknowledged to me that she had been unkind. I did not contact her because I wanted her to apologize; I only tried to connect with her to say good-bye since I had not been aware she was sick. Yes, regardless of my past interactions with Edie having been negative, I still felt guilty since I did not make it easy for Edie to be nice to me. I guess I wanted closure and I needed to connect to also show my desire to make amends as well.

At a near-death experience conference, a woman who had died and returned back to earth, shared that she was shown images from her childhood. In particular, she was shown a time when she had been mean to a girl when she was just 8 years old. She said the experience was given to her to teach her how much she had hurt someone's feeling even at that age and how it had impacted the other little girl. This woman was sent back to earth after a near-death experience with a true connection to an enlightened spirit. She now had a mission assigned to her from the Other Side beings she interacted with when going through that near-death moment. She was asked to tell her story to try and transform how humans here interact and treat each other. She also stated she had seen how the world would end but was not permitted to share that information at all. Her response was that we are not permitted to know many things about life after death and how the world will end, but during our stay on earth, we are obligated to treat each other fairly and with respect.

A Friend from Graduate School- a fellow Chronic Fatigue Sufferer-Susan

When I was in my second year of my Ph.D. program, I had contracted Lyme disease, which had been diagnosed as "stress" by a doctor. Unfortunately, I had been not able to do my early morning four-mile runs each day due to extreme fatigue, which was supposedly stress induced. I had migraines, terrible pain in my joints and the worst part was not one bit of desire to exercise. I almost failed out of my Ph.D. program due to fatigue, but fortunately, I was at the writing stage of my dissertation and was able to work from home.

A fellow student, Susan, who I was very fond of as a beautiful spirit in this world, also contracted Chronic Fatigue. Actually two other women in my Ph.D. program were diagnosed as well, so possibly the stress related to being a student, holding down a job and taking care of children was all too much on our bodies. I will only state that a total of four women in this doctoral program were eventually diagnosed with chronic fatigue, which was probably a burn out syndrome from trying to balance out the stress.

Susan was also a very high energy person and a volunteer for an AIDS group. We were both teaching a course while in graduate school and although she did not have children and a husband, she was in a committed relationship with another woman. She was open as a lesbian and quite a role model for those students who had preconceived notions of what a lesbian was or looked like; not all were butch stereotypically gay and Susan shattered that mold.

71

The year I was writing up my research, Susan had become very sick with her chronic fatigue syndrome and fibromyalgia. Since neither disease could be treated to the point of a cure, it was a frustrating syndrome to have to live with on many levels. I had suffered for five years in agony with a bedridden life and my family fell apart around me. I then had heard from my colleague that Susan had committed suicide. I was in disbelief but somehow understood the rationale on some level. I knew what it was like to have this disease and be sick all the time, no energy and in bed non-stop.

Susan had been such an upbeat, positive, high-energy and sparkly person and was well loved by all who knew her. I enjoyed her so much as a fellow spirit and dedicated AIDS educator. We had gotten to know each other when Susan came to guest speak in my classes on human sexuality about lesbian health issues. Susan was a wonderful kind person who had given so much of her life to the AIDS crisis and lesbian health issues, that it was so hard to accept her death.

My colleague described the sad funeral day as people being in constant tears and disbelief. I could not attend due to my own illnesses. It was a shock and a tragedy to all and I needed to know why Susan chose that path and again, say good-bye to her. I just was so upset by her "giving up" and "giving in" to this beautiful life she had lived. I was told that her suicide note said she could not go on living with chronic fatigue anymore, that she was just a shell of her former self. Boy, did I know the feeling having spent five years in bed with the same disease syndrome which resulted in my divorce and husband walking out due to my illnesses. So, my way of providing some insight was to contact her on the Other Side.

Heavenly Session with Susan

Feeling compelled to make sense of her suicide I wanted to connect with her. I asked **W** to track her down and again, I gave her little information about Susan or her suicide. Susan appeared to **W** with her bright smile being transmitted through the portal. **W** immediately stated she is smiling and that was the way Susan always interacted with the world. Susan then told **W** she could not take the drastic change in her life after being so sick in bed for so long. Susan, like myself when experiencing the peak of chronic fatigue and felt she had let so many people down by her illness. I understood that emotion of having to cancel out an incredible teaching career at a medical school due to my illnesses.

Susan understood clearly the implications of her suicide and according to Susan, she was shown all the other good deeds she would have completed if she had stayed on this side of the world. Susan only stated that

"She knew her partner was devastated at being left behind by her suicide and that she witnessed the funeral with the tears of so many who were in pain."

Reflection:

Suicide deaths are instances that do seem to challenge those enlightened spirits on the Other Side immensely. Whomever it is that guides us through the process of learning about our past life on earth is very specific in dealing with a suicide death once one gets to the Other Side. I don't know why this topic is so challenging to Other Side spirits since I would almost seem to think they should know it is going to happen. Most individuals who do "hasten their lives" do so out of some agony internally they are experiencing, not really as a selfish act. Yes, they want to be away from the pain in this life and possibly, they were not prepared to deal with the many negatives this earthly life has to offer. I can only assume that the deeds assigned to a person when on earth are not completed in that life cycle, somehow upsets a universal theme for that person's life. As with my cousin's suicide, it was a very negative moment in time when we connected to him as he was raked over the carpet for his suicide. I can't explain why there were these differences in the connection with the Other Side but it was yet, another learning experience for both **W** and me.

The Native American Healer- A Sudden, Unexpected Death

I had participated in some sessions with a body works healer who performed a combination of massage, chiropractic adjustments and some spiritual healing. It had transformed my life because of the spirituality and healings for me through this specific Native American man. I was hoping to get relief from my pain syndrome through a natural process and bodyworks methods did accomplish this on some level. This healer man (okay you may not believe this but I swear I just received a message from him in my mind that said he did not want his name used, so my apologies for referring to him as Native American healer man). I don't question this message, well yes I do because I am not use to getting these messages, but am respectful of the communication that was transmitted.

The healer man, P, was gifted beyond most people I have known, in mind, spirit and body. He presented a transformative gift to the world. He was an empath, a spirited soul from the past and yes, an indigo if you read the definitions in the first chapter, this makes sense to you at this point. The Native American Healer had connected with me and two of my children with some intense spiritual insights and used his physical healing power to help all three of us. He adjusted the umbilical connections from birth that supposedly interfered with my emotions that blocked my chakras and continued to block a healing. If you are interested in understanding this process more, please read up on the power of bodyworks. The healer man had just been in Philadelphia two weeks earlier offering these sessions and I had attended one with him. However, at that session, out of the four I had prior, he appeared to me to be of very low energy and not at a high level of interactions that I had grown to appreciate so much for his past healings. I had received a call from a friend who stated he had died very suddenly. I was saddened, upset by the loss and yes, needed to connect because he was truly an inspiration to me to move on further with my own work in healings.

After a further conversation with his close friend, I learned that P had died from a heart attack during the night in his sleep. I do hope I die that peacefully and feel no pain since I have witnessed some disturbing deaths as a RN. So, I chose to ask **W** to be connected to the now deceased healer, and at the precise moment of the connection **W** had found him in a circle with Native American shamans and healers. I reiterate, I told **W** nothing of this man's heritage or that he was a healer of Native American origin. Yet, she found him sitting in a Shaman circle discussing the needs of the world with other Native American spiritual guides. According to **W**, we had interrupted him in an intense learning session with the elders, then he asked if we could wait a moment.

The healer man actually turned around to acknowledge **W** out of a courtesy since they were deep in conversation when we arrived in that dimension in time. So, we waited? What were we doing to say no, we could not wait? It took only 10 seconds for him to ask permission to connect with us and then he turned his attention to **W**'s communication portal. This is the second time I found someone in a circle of other side entities who were either guiding someone, or as in the case of my cousin's suicide, informing him of the pain he left behind and their intense disapproval of this suicide process.

My first question to this healer was what happened that you died so suddenly? He replied,

"I was just as surprised, I awoke on the Other Side not realizing at first I even had passed away!!

Somehow, his heart had given up on him at the age of 50 he then said,

"Can you imagine my surprise to have woken up and found myself on the other side and realized I had actually died"?

He told me to stay with taking care of my body through healings, and to continue to have my daughter work on her condition. Again, nothing more exciting occurred in that session other than above, but I requested he continue to guide me to help me get through this side of life. He agreed to do what he could from afar.

Reflection:

I don't know if and how spirits on the Other Side can help us or are even permitted to do so once they die. I only know that my father said he would come to my mom in her dreams to try and guide her into accepting being transferred to a long-term care facility. My father also told me he often comes and sits on my blue chair in my living room to try and comfort me when upset. I can't expound on any further details of what our deceased ones can do for us, I only know what has been shared during my contact with both pets and humans through these medium exchanges. So for those of you who feel the sadness and despair of having had a loved one pass, my only words of hope are that they can visit this side and be with us, so please know they are still with you.

My Grandfather: An Uninvited Connection

I had never met any of my grandfathers since they all had died when I was an infant. My paternal grandfather was supposedly an alcoholic, very mean and had died young due to a liver problem. As noted in my father's connection, this seemed to be the rationale he made for some of his own distant behaviors, having not had a caring/gentle father while in his childhood or young adult life.

I did not even think to ask to speak to any of my deceased grandfathers since I never met them and could not envision the benefit of that contact. Honestly, it never occurred to me that I could connect with someone I never met. During another Other Side session, a man came through out of the blue. **W** tried to describe him from what she was seeing about his hair and features, but it did not ring a bell to me as anyone I knew. I only heard a few brief sentences about either of my grandfathers in my entire life. My paternal grandmother did not speak of him often due to the sad state of his alcoholism and how he ruined most lives of those he crossed paths with when on earth. I felt a bit cheated by not having any grandfathers to get to know, but my grandmothers were both incredible women and wonderful role models. I had no male role models then to fill the gap where my father could not be a male figure. I didn't think this paternal grandfather would have been the one candidate to help me out at all due to his own problems. I do believe, if I had a grandfather to experience life with as another male role model, that it may have helped me understand men a bit more later on in life. The lack of contact with my dad just never had me learn about males as husbands, partners, fathers or any role due to my sheer lack of exposure in a family setting.

I can't remember who I was speaking to on the Other Side when suddenly the medium stated, "Someone else is coming through." She started to describe him to me stating he had gray hair and was elderly, and then said, no it is a woman I think the name coming to me is Angela. Well, I had a cousin Angela who was still very much alive. My paternal grandfather was named Angelo, so I stated, could it be a male and be Angelo? As soon as the name was off my tongue, the entity starting bobbing their head yes to confirm to my medium I was on the right track.

"He is shaking his head yes and smiling".

I was so floored, how on earth did a grandfather I never met come through on a session I was not even trying to connect with him? This was one connection that threw me off a bit. Angelo then said that,

"He was so very proud of me and all my accomplishments, and that other members of the family were witness to my work as a nurse and with helping people, especially people with AIDS".

I did not know what to say. I was not asking for praise but it was sure inspiring to know that those on the Other Side witnessed the good I had done. That was about the extent of the exchange, but again, one never can predict what will come of those other side connections once the portal is opened.

Reflection

I have no idea how they, on the other side, view us here on earth or see what we experience. I only know that this connection had not been requested, was with a grandfather I never met and now he was stating how proud he was of me with no other prior connection. That was all that was shared by him and then the image was gone.

My Aunt Butch: Heaven is just beautiful!!

I was close to an aunt who was from the Deep South and had married my father's brother, John. Aunt Butch was called Butch since during WW II she became a Rosie-the-Riveter sort of woman doing hard work on airplanes to help with the war effort. I really enjoyed my Aunt Butch and she had been a role model for me in some way. Aunt Butch had finished college and was now a math teacher in a school. These paternal relatives were from Virginia and visited each Thanksgiving. It was a very joyous time since I saw my four cousins who only made it to Philadelphia once a year for the Thanksgiving parade.

I had a very strong connection to Aunt Butch since she somehow came across to me even as a child as an intelligent being. I don't know why or how I picked that up as different from most of my own family members, but Aunt Butch had a self-confidence and persona that I assumed her college years and as a professional, had which made her stand out from all my other relatives. Note, not one in my immediate adult family had ever gone to college, and my Aunt Butch, was a married into the family relative. Over the years we kept in touch and after her husband died; she was quite home bound due to a foot deformity problem. I called her once a month and just got caught up with all the family news and she also was proud of my educational pursuits and work with AIDS.

When I heard she had died, I felt quite sad since I had not spoken with her for a few months due to my own issues of not coping well with a personal situation. I really did want to say good-bye to her and let her know I was sorry I had not been in touch prior to her death. It also meant a great deal to me to know she, as an intelligent and educated person, may give me some other insight into the Other Side experience. Aunt Butch had been a devout Southern Baptist and I was certainly interested in finding out what she was experiencing on the

Other Side. The medium connected with Aunt Butch immediately and I apologized for loosing contact with her. Aunt Butch and I used to talk about religion a great deal, so naturally the question I asked was,

"What is heaven like"? Are you with Uncle John?

Aunt Butch only responded,

"It is so beautiful here, just absolutely beautiful".

So I guess she was in one of those good places and seemed happy now that she was with her husband John. No other words were spoken to describe Heaven, so maybe it was not permitted to give out the details. I was just happy we connected, that she was okay and that she said heaven was beautiful, coming from a devout Christian, it meant a great deal to me.

Reflection:

I can't say how long a transition takes if one can go directly to the heavenly place or if all beings have to go first to the "place of learning" about their negative past deeds. I do not have a time line for how long it takes for any deceased soul to move on to either the learning in-between place or when they actually move to the heavenly place on the other side. It is just as individual of a process as each person is as an individual when reaching the other side. At least that is my take on the matter. **W** responded,

"There are some things about the Other Side we are not supposed to know about"

Wow, coming from **W** I knew it was a powerful statement that told me not to push too hard on this subject whenever I did connect with the Other Side. But, this next experience with the other side is one that is not at all a positive one. I am asking you to be prepared for a very, scary, sad and complicated story. I hesitated whether to put this next session even in this book but I want you to know that this type of experience is rare. So, please don't be too freaked out by the connection and the possible dark side of dying. This one case study deserves an entire chapter on its own due to the combined issues it raises and the degree, length of time and energy it took to all is resolved.

Chapter VII

The Lost Soul of a Young Girl

I worked as a RN in an outpatient clinic and one of my patients had a tragedy happen that just took his entire life away from him in an instant. I had known D for over a year and felt I had a good connection with him as an occupational health patient on multiple levels. He came to the clinic for numerous chronic health issues and I was always willing to spend extra time to just chat about our children and life at the ranch (or workplace) so to speak.

D had a young daughter who was a slow learner. His daughter was also a very morbidly obese young girl of 22. D's daughter had been teased horribly when in school and it was hard on her since the nuns had very little patience. D then took her out of Catholic school and put her in a public school during the first grade. She grew up and leaned some basic skills so was able to get a job as a file clerk when she turned 18. D's daughter was working part-time and productive but still living at home. D loved that he still had a child at home and she needed the extra support of living with her parents. D's daughter, being the baby, had requested to have the type of surgery her older sister had, the stomach reassignment surgery that helped obese people lose weight.

D was hesitant to go forward with this surgery for his daughter and objected from the start. His other daughter, who is not mentally challenged, had done quite well with the surgical procedure and was successful in losing weight fairly quickly. The youngest daughter just was relentless in her pursuit of wanting to lose weight and not be teased any more. Even though she was mentally challenged, she was able to recognize the way people treated her and looked at her because of her obesity.

D had not mentioned his daughter's upcoming surgery to me at any time prior so I was not even aware it had happened until the tragic repercussions of that surgery occurred. D's younger daughter had lost over 90 lbs in six months and was so happy she had been successful. D stated that his daughter often complained of being tired after the surgery and slept a bit more, but otherwise, she went out to work each day and was again, a productive citizen and oh so very happy about her weight loss.

One day I had expected D to stop by for his usual clinic check-up, and was informed by his supervisor that D's daughter had died suddenly during the night. There was neither foul play nor any drugs involved nor was it a suicide, nothing at all could be accounted for at the time of the death. Yet, how does a 22-year-old young lady in the prime of her life, just suddenly die in her sleep and is now, gone.

Unfortunately, her father found her in her bed dead and already blue when he went to wake her for work the next morning. D tried to do mouth to mouth for over fifteen minutes while he waited for an ambulance to arrive to the third floor of his home. D, as the one parent who objected so much to the surgery, was now blaming himself for her death since he felt from the start he should not have permitted it to happen. He kept saying he had a bad feeling about the surgery from the get go but eventually caved in to his daughter's desire to lose weight and feel better about herself. D's daughter autopsy results demonstrated that his daughter had died from a complication of a clot in her heart that caused her chronic tiredness and had been missed by the surgeons during both the pre-op evaluation and post-op check-ups.

D came back to work a month later and was a shell of the man who he used to be. The former, strong, powerful union leader in the company now cried most of the day while he tried to perform his maintenance duties. D came to the health center at lunch each day just because he needed a place to cry and vent his emotions. Each day for over a month D would come to my office and he would talk through his pain. I was not a therapist but only an RN who could listen well and help support him on some level. As an Emapth, I felt his pain deeply and as a parent, cried my heart out each day as well. I too feared I might one day have to experience something so sad and tragic. D had shared with me at a number of these sessions that he felt his daughter was still with him in some way and D stated, I keep hearing my daughter speak to me and says

"It is so cold and so dark, what has happened"?

I was certain that D's grief had him hearing voices and had recommended he see a counselor. After another few weeks of D coming to my office and being in such anguish and pain, I felt I had to do something else now to help him. I informed D about my medium connection and how she had assisted me with coping with deceased relatives and in particular, my father. D was not sure he could handle such an exchange, and being Catholic, he was not sure he necessarily believed that communication with the dead was not a sin. The Bible does state in a few of the verses that one should not use mediums or talk to the dead. D gave me permission to connect with his daughter and gave me a photo of her so I could help the medium with the connection. I explained to **W** how grief stricken the father was and that he kept blaming himself. **W** said she was okay with trying to connect, but not even **W** was in any way prepared with what would happen in this particular incident and tragedy.

The Session: A shock to Me and **W**

I was on the phone with the medium and had the photo of the young girl in front of me so I could provide a description of her. It took a bit longer than usual to find her and then suddenly **W** became very, very intensely upset. Her words were the following:

"This spirit is much stressed and has not crossed over, this spirit is very confused, and this spirit is still wandering around on this side of the planet and is definitely deceased. Oh my God this poor child is so stressed out and confused and keeps stating repeatedly .... it is so cold and dark."

These were the exact words her father kept hearing as well and I had not shared with **W** about these words shared by D to me the week prior. **W** tried to reach the girl and explain to her that she had died in her sleep from the complications of the surgery, although it was two months later. The young woman was not sure she actually heard **W** correctly and was still very confused. She stated she could not leave her "poppy" or Daddy, alone and that D needed her still here on this side. I actually intervened for the first time ever in talking directly to the spirit by trying to explain her death was a result of the surgery. I tried to remind her that the surgery made her so tired and that it was her heart's reaction to the surgery, and not her own failure or fault, that the surgery did not work at all.

W asked me, do you know of any of her relatives that are on the other side we can call them to the portal to convince this child to cross over to the light? Well, hadn't we had a similar experience when Squirty the pup would not leave me to cross over and we had to get Misty, our recently deceased dog to help with that going to the light? God

Bless Squirty for teaching not only the professors at Penn that animal communicators could play an integral role in communicating with deceased pets but now after our Squirty experience we were more prepared with what to do when all else fails. These two cases were similar in that a spirit is still not wanting to cross over and chooses to remain on this side due to loyalty, confusion or just not realizing it was their time and in disbelief they had died.

When I first met D, he shared that his Mother had died a few years back, so I told **W** there was a grandmother on the paternal side that had crossed. She managed to connect with the deceased grandmother by some basic description I remembered about this her grandmother being small, obese and an unusually light-haired Italian woman. **W** then actually described the grandmother back to me in detail as she then appeared at the portal of light. **W** requested that the grandmother assist in helping her granddaughter to cross over to the light. Not too many other dead people who would have taken on this role from the other side, so there was no doubt it was the paternal grandmother of D. Why some type of assistance had not been attempted prior by the family on the Other Side to help this child pass over I do not understand at all. Why did it take a medium, a complete stranger like me and a two month delay for this to happen? Unfortunately, the daughter did not want to leave her father and was pleading to remain on this side out of sheer agony of having to leave him.

The daughter then shared a visualization to the medium how she was presently now in the living room of her old home and with her father at that precise moment. D was sitting in a recliner chair with the TV on and had fallen asleep, according to the medium's description of the scene. The daughter was now sitting on the arm side of the chair and then just leaned over and kissed her Dad on his bald head. She then spoke up saying how she was confused about it all and somehow did not know she was to go to the light.

W kept repeating to her that she had to go to the light that she could not stay on this side. When the child learned that her grandmother was waiting for her, it still took some tough love to get the daughter to leave her father. The daughter finally conceded to go to the light, but not without one more surprise for both **W** and I. **W** reported to me what she was observing as the daughter left the house and moved toward the portal. **W** could see the daughter's spirit going toward the light and moving away from this world. **W** was so relieved at that moment since **W** was able to feel all the pain and agony the daughter was experiencing both physically and mentally. The entire session took almost twenty minutes from start to finish which is an enormous amount of time for one medium's energy to be spent in connecting to an open portal, two people, one on earth and the other, the grandmother in the heavens above.

Suddenly, **W** actually screamed out …

*"No, no, she stated in a panic, she has come back down the portal and is now with her father again in the living room. **W** said the daughter has slipped back through the portal to earth".*

The child went gently up to her father and kissed his bald head, then took her hand and patted him on his bald head a few times. She stated repeatedly, "I love you Pappy. I love you my Pappy!". **W** was able to see the grandmother waiting at the light and described the grandmother to me as very short, very obese woman and with light brown, almost blonde wavy type hair. I could not imagine anyone would try to impersonate a grandmother on the other side! Finally, the drama was over. I was so upset and overwhelmed by this entire exchange that I was crying in disbelief. Why had I been motivated to intervene, was it meant to be for me to help this spirit as a story to tell to you now in this book?

W was totally exhausted and wiped out from the experience again, all of this was over the phone. Not one other side connections with **W** ever took place in person, ever. How gifted can one person be to be able to connect to all of these beings through some outer limits of connectivity? The string theory must be right and quantum physics has certainly made the particles of our being capable of connecting through all types of processes.

The Aftermath: Facing Her Dad

Now, I went to work the next morning and waited for D to arrive at his office. As soon as I saw his car, I stopped him and asked to speak with him immediately. D was a bit confused since I never showed up at his office shop at 6 a.m. We sat in my car and I was quite nervous about having to share this not-so-good news to D. I began by asking D what he did last night. D stated that he fell asleep in his living room on his recliner and had a dream about his daughter patting him on the head and saying she loved him.

D stated, *"That was her special way of saying good night to me, a pat on the head and I love you".*

My heart sank and I was so afraid to tell him the experience I had with his daughter and the medium exchange. I went on to describe the Other Side session and D was absolutely furious, as well as in a rage and angry with God. He asked how could God let a mentally challenged girl stay on this side and suffer as she did, how could God not show her the way? What kind of God would let this happen? I had no answers but stated that his mother had helped her. He asked how were you sure if was my mother? I replied by giving specific details about the color of her hair, his size and her weight. D was astounded by the accuracy of that description and no longer questioned the exchange. He was still very upset his daughter suffered but happy to know she had gone to the Other Side and was with his mother.

Reflection:

I had chosen to get involved in this case, only trying to help, not knowing the complex nature of the exchange. I am not sure it was a good idea to share it with D since he will now have to live with those thoughts for the rest of his life here on earth. Although I realize the benefit of helping his daughter reach the other side was a good thing and definitely outweighed D's emotions. But having D be so angry with God and just so upset his daughter had suffered, was a challenge I hope not to have to occur any time again in my life.

This case is rare and according to the medium, it was the first one she had ever experienced. Out of the rest of my Other Side communications, I did not have this occur again. But, knowing it could happen, both with Squirty waiting for me and this young girl not wanting to leave her Father, had taught me a valuable lesson. I know I want to go directly to the light and not linger here. But why does it still happen? I have to accept that these types of occurrences can occur when souls and spirits are stressed and not prepared to leave this earth for some odd reason. Maybe that is what a ghost really is? Some beings are wandering this world of the living when they are suppose to go to the light. Maybe this is the purgatory that awaits us all for the dark hole of spiraling through to the light may be the only way some will enter the other side. I can't believe it has to be based on good deeds or not so good deeds on this earth. This occurrence can happen just from some freakish, sudden death when a soul has no time to prepare or adjust to their demise. It is a rare occurrence in the universe. I believe any medium does not want to have to experience this type of exchange if it can be avoided due to the stress it places on their psyche.

For those of you expecting to be relieved by these case studies, please accept my apology if I have upset you. Know that this was a rare occurrence and was the only one both the medium and I experienced.

I want you not to worry that a loved one is wandering on this side after death. If you do have a concern, please seek out a reputable psychic to check on it. I don't want this lost spirit event to deter you from doing what you believe it best, based on your own unique experiences after the loss of a loved one.

Chapter VIII

The Guest Speaker-
Terry's life with AIDS

I met Terry when I was working on an AIDS education research project for my doctorate work. He was giving a presentation about AIDS and his life at Philadelphia University in 1986. I had been promoting AIDS safe-sex seminars at Temple University and other local high schools, when I had heard about his powerful presentations about AIDS. After witnessing Terry's story about his one night stand as a heterosexual male, resulting in contracting the HIV virus and AIDS, I knew he would have a great impact on the audience that I was working with for the college/graduate students I was teaching at Penn. He had a better statement to make than me and I was readily accepting of whatever would work to get through to these white, heterosexual, middle class students who thought AIDS was for the poor, IV drug user or prostitute.

Terry and I did join forces and did more than present to over 100 groups. We fell in love with each other's spirit and commitment to AIDS prevention. It was a difficult but a necessary lesson to learn to just say no to his charisma. Being married with children made it obviously a definite no as well, plus it was against our own principles as AIDS educators. My husband also admired Terry and knew I loved him, platonically speaking, but it did not help our situation that my husband became jealous over time. It was obvious to all that our intensity of finding a true, soul mate and connected love impacted how we interacted with each other. But no sexual, or even physical actions took place, other than on his deathbed.

Terry died a year after I had known him and fortunately, I spent the last night of his life with him in a hospital bed, literally sleeping with him fully clothed in my nursing scrubs. Terry died an hour after I left him in peace and out of pain. It was and has been, one of the most tragic experiences of my life, emotionally and spiritually.

The Other Side Connection: Terry and the Afterlife Lessons I was to Learn

I had waited almost 15 years after Terry's death to connect with him, only because it was not until the year 2001 that I made the discovery that **W** could do readings with humans as well as pets. My father was the first, which was a total of two connections and the other connections were just once. Terry's was one of the most consistent connections I had, having had three exchanges with him before he moved on to an incarnation or sorts.

My medium stated upfront that she was not sure she could connect due to his possibly having already moved on to another life. According to her, one can move on and it can be in a form of reincarnation depending on where they were in the process of the life experience in their own time frame both on earth and the other side. **W** did connect (as she has always come through) and found Terry sitting at a desk typing on a computer. He turned around to acknowledge the connection and was filled with joy it was me. He said,

"I am working on the screenplay"

Which of course I was doing this as well from this side of the planet. Only Terry and I knew about this screenplay, so I realized again, this was a validation about the connection that meant nothing to the medium as she relayed the words to me.

Terry stated,

"I don't want you to stress yourself out over the screenplay, and it is not the right time for this story to be told anyway. There is a great deal of AIDS education being done now, so don't push yourself to exhaustion to complete this promise".

I said that I would continue on with the screenplay and he said,

"You will know when the time is right and I will be guiding you from this side."

When Terry presented in his my classes on AIDS for my students, he always spoke about what his expectations were of life after death. Terry would explain to the audience that he was a Catholic and was not worried about the other side or a heaven experience. He would state that "I am looking forward to meeting my Creator".

So, I had to ask once we connected, how is your experience of "God"? Terry replied in a single sentence that shocked me into a reality like no other. Terry replied with deliberate diplomacy,

"It is not like we learned in Catholic school"

That was it, he was not permitted to say another word, and it was a moment in time that has impacted me with all that I do now and one of the main reasons I am working on with this book. You have to draw your own conclusions from all the case studies I am sharing with you from the honest and blatant harsh realities to the beauty of the experiences as they happened to me.

The medium responded again,

"There are some things we are not to know as yet on this side, Barbara, so that was all he was going to say on the subject".

We parted that session with me requesting to Terry and the medium that we could possibly meet again, and it was agreed that we would. That third session turned out to be the last as Terry had decided to give me some more words of encouragement about the screenplay but also told the medium he was now with friends and moving on to another realm. It was hard to realize it was the end of that contact but again, I know I will see him again in some spirit form or entity when I cross over as well.

Reflection

I guess I am fortunate to have received that statement about God (just not being exactly what we were taught) which led me to question even more of what is and what is not on the Other Side. The session ended with Terry turning back to his computer and no other words were shared. I was elated by my connections with Terry and happy he chose to move on to another realm of existence where he would be loved and hopefully be reincarnated to experience the joys of Fatherhood that he so much missed due to AIDS.

My Mother's Death

This last connection with my mother has been my last contact now for two years. My mother, who died December 8, 2009, had completed a circle of life for me that has lead me down this road to writing the book. I had used another medium for this connection, since **W** had requested she not continue on with my readings. **W** felt, and I respected her feelings, that we had run our course and she wanted me to back off being so dependent on her for readings with her in particular. Yes, admittedly, I was calling her a great deal for my everyday pet issues. **W** stated that I had the ability to reach my pets and that I needed to practice it. **W** had given me a few pointers and an incredible amount of her time and energy. She was a mentor of sorts and we closed that chapter of my life.

I have since, referred others to **W** for pet communications, but she firmly stated she would not be doing any human connections in the future. Whatever her rationale, I don't question, but I was fortunate to find the Psychic Twins, who are mediums as well and spiritual guides. My connection with The Twins, Linda and Terry Jamison, was mostly about my spiritual guidance for the future with the screenplay and this book. I also sought out the twins for a different reason than when using **W**, the twins were able to predict some future events that made them on a different plane that **W**. You will see the similarities, especially when I connected with my mother.

Death of My Mother: A Difficult One to Witness

My mother had laid for 10 days unconscious with her bodily functions shutting down one by one. Blue arms and legs searched restlessly for the red blood cells to revive them, but to no avail. As the extremities are the farthest body parts from the central blood organ the heart, they were the visual demonstrations that her body was now trying to sustain the vital organs. Even at 84, my mother's body held on for 10 days after a massive stroke. She wasn't ready to let go which confused me since we tried to decide together, as her children, her wishes for a non-assisted death.

The three children had decided against neurosurgery to clear the clot in her head from the stroke with some reluctance. But knowing she had been through four hospitalizations in one year due to a fracture of her arm, two fractures of her hips and another fall, we did what was in her best interest. We did not believe she would want another long rehab post stroke, and her wishes to my brother in her last will were clear about this last struggle. Fortunately, we had a medical directive from her written five years prior that alleviated the decision making at such a tragic time. I recommend to all above the age of sixty-five to have a medical directive and last will made up with specific plans for your dying needs and use of mechanical and pharmaceutical interventions. The family behind needs this document to heed your wishes, so please make certain you are prepared legally and morally to handle this last call to arms.

We sat vigil for days around her bed and as time went on, my sister and brother had to return to work. I happen to be in between jobs at that time, so I was there most of the day time, just holding her hand. My mother was conscious enough the first few days after her stroke to squeeze back tightly and even reached out for a hand to hold. She had a desperation in her reaching almost sensing it was her last connection with us and this earthly plane. She had some anxiety about death, I am certain. I urged her on whispering words of encouragement so she could join her family members. Being the 15th child, she was the last of her lineage to die and I know many of her siblings were waiting to greet her. I knew I would speak to her again through an Other Side contact, so I was okay with this final stage, or at least I thought I could handle it as a nurse and daughter.

My experiences over the past ten years of other side conversations with friends and family, had reassured me that I would connect again with my mother and know she was okay and happy. I would reach out to my medium friends in a few weeks so I could be certain that my mother had caught up with my dad and all the family members who had left her so many years ago. My mother had missed so many life experiences with her husband for his death was so sudden at age 55. My mom was only 45 when she became a young widow and then, one by one her other 14 siblings passed away and she was the last, being the baby and all. It was hard for her those last two years as dementia took over and she lost some of her independence. I was actually happy knowing she was going to a place that I felt was a secure one and full of joy for her to experience after a long life of poverty, joy and sadness.

The Final Day:

The nurses called me as I was just walking out the door of my home on December 8 to come to the nursing facility immediately. The RN stated that my mother would not make it through the day. I arrived in time to sit with her for the final hour of her life as she labored with her breathing known as agonal breathing. It is difficult to watch because we are consciously witnessing her body's last fight to stay alive with oxygen being depleted gradually minute by minute. The labored breaths are about six per hour, which come after long intervals of pausing, so each one may be the last. It is a difficult time for even a daughter who is a nurse, it was my own Mommy dying in front of me.

When her eyes flew open with her last breath, she looked upward to the heavens knowing someone was reaching out to guide her there. I tried to make eye contact with her at that moment, but her pupils were so focused on the heavens, she did not acknowledge my presence. I said

"Mom, just go now, please, go be with Daddy".

Her last breath was most difficult to witness for me as she sighed the relief of passing of a life that was definitely not an easy one for her. Even as a nurse who had experienced bedside death sessions for over thirty years, I found it difficult to accept this was my mother who I had just spent the last moments of life pass away to the next. My main concern was that she had suffered in any way that last day, but I was later reassured by an anesthesiologist friend of mine that the unconscious brain has taken care of the pain when in a coma.

I sat in silence as the calmness of her body was felt and I shared the peace of her mind. I did not go and get the charge nurse to confirm her death since I already had checked the pulse. It was that quiet time and the peace of a death that we shared alone that helped me with my difficult memories of her body's deterioration and last breaths the previous hours. Someone came into the room and took out her roommate, who was sequestered off behind a curtain. Fortunately, her roommate was totally deaf and had no understanding of what had just transpired. After the nurse's aide realized my mother had passed, from a mere nod by me, in her crossing the room, she then sent for the charge nurse to announce the death. The charge nurse walked in to do her duty as the death certificate and time of death had to be noted and signed.

The nurse gently placed a stethoscope on my Mother's chest to be certain there was no heartbeat. The she shook her head very slightly, "yes", to confirm the death with the utmost respect. After she walked out of the room, a beautiful white hue glowed around my mother and filled the space where my mother lay. Her face looked angelic, peaceful and finally at rest. After a long life of being financially poor and a woman with no husband to share her years from age 45 to 85, I was certain she would be much happier on the Other Side. I was so relieved when I sensed her presence above me in the room floating upward and said,

"Have fun with daddy".

I looked upward as I could feel her leaving and heading toward the light, she was ready to be set free. I was elated as her spirit was filled with such joy. I later discovered that this was truly a gift so very few witness at the moment of death, since we so readily as humans have to leave the place of the death out of just sheer sorrow. If we can only learn to stay and be with our deceased person or pet long enough to feel that spirit be uplifted into the heavens through the portal of light, it would give to many a beautiful memory to have in their mind from a death that can be so painful to witness.

Post Death Contact

When I contacted the Psychic Twins, Terry and Linda Jamison, it was about a month after my Mother's death. I just had to check in on my mom even though I was sure she was happy. However, the beginning of the session was a bit confusing for them. The first thought they shared was "why are we seeing a lasagna pan"? Linda said she has never had anyone from the Other Side ever share food with them, so they hesitated to even tell me what they were seeing. Well, I knew that it was my mother's way of saying it is me and to authenticate the exchange, especially since it only the third time I had used the Twins for my connections.

My mother's favorite meal to make for our family day celebrations was lasagna. Over the Christmas celebration, birthdays, Easter and even Thanksgiving, along with a turkey, we had lasagna. The twin, Linda, who received this visual message was even embarrassed thinking she had misunderstood the visual message. I am so pleased and grateful she was open enough to share a questionable exchange from the Other Side. Then the other twin stated,

"I won't question any message or visual I get again from the Other Side, this was a learning session for me as well".

The twins mentioned that my mother was now with a German Shepherd dog on the Other Side. That was her childhood dog, Bessie. I ask you, how on earth could the mediums have known that detail of her childhood unless they were speaking and observing my mother on the Other Side. There is no Facebook, email, computer documentation or any other means by which anyone, other than close family, would know she had a dog named Bessie when she was six years old. Again, a validation for me it was my mom and she was happy. My mother also shared with The Twins that she was with "Pat"; they asked, was this her husband? They mentioned my mother was in the presence of her "parents." I was so relieved all was well with my mom and now I could move past my sorrow at the pain I witnessed during the death-bed event. It was just a month later after her last day of life and I was relieved immensely. Yes, I mourned and missed her yet, knowing she was happy on the Other Side with my father and family, took my pain away immensely.

I was at peace with her death and was able to share the above new information with my sister, who is also a firm believer of Other Side communications. Fortunately, my children were believers and happy to hear the above. We were all healed by this two-minute experience with the Other Side connection.

Reflection: So, at age 60 I now had two deceased parents back together on the Other Side. I was pleased their new lives could start again in whatever direction or journey they would choose. I have no reason to reconnect with my parents again at this time and can let go of that part of my life with such a sense of fulfillment and closure.

Chapter IX

Some Science to Ponder

Where do we go after we die and in what form do we exist?

The opportunity to have an Other Side contact is a gift from the universe to us here as earth bound beings. There is a reason, I am sure, that the universe has provided us with individuals who are psychic. Psychics are endowed with a multitude of gifts as well as mediumship capabilities. However mediumship abilities are not gifts that all psychics share in common. The psychic who is a medium has a unique gift that permits them to act as a conduit or go between for humans to speak to our deceased loved ones. One of the mediums I utilized was also an animal communicator yet, it is not common for mediums to connect to earth bound and deceased animals alike. Another medium I had the privilege to work with could do intensive body healings, speak to animals and serve in a mediumship capacity. From my experience and in what I have read in the limited studies on this topic, this was a unique set of gifts too. Fortunately additional research is being funded to study mediumship as I was notified during the last week of writing this book. Funding needs to devoted to the study of mediumship using both brain wave connections through PET scans combined with quantum theories such as that at the Princeton Lab on Cognitive Studies.

Part of my learning curve in experiencing these medium connections was one which resulted in an intense questioning with a need to understand why and how mediumship can occur. I want to share the connections I have made regarding mediumship with you through the writing of this last chapter. My interest is centered around the age-old question of where do we go after we die and what happens to us after death? Although I have had only a glimpse into what heaven is like, through the eyes of the deceased spirits, I am still not able to answer those fundamental questions. However, I am attempting in this chapter to answer a few questions about how the medium connects to the deceased, what form do we take after we death and how is the information accessed after we die. The following summary is taken from connections I made in my mind from this twenty year study, as well as from a few quantum theories I have researched for this book. Please know they are very fundamental in nature and require a more rigorous scientific investigation through further collaboration with other researchers.

Psychic medium and Other Side beings may be able to communicate through an opening or portal yet to be identified. It may also be just as likely that there is no actual separate dimension or portal at all between the dead and living. Do deceased beings co-exist or just visit earth's dimension in a spirit form that can be accessed only by mediumship and psychic abilities? Can we as scientist eventually figure out the process as to how the deceased and medium connect? What I believe psychic mediums can accomplish, from my limited experiences, is to make a connection to a deceased entity through both the memories from their earth time after death and also connect to the spirit in their present state of existence in the afterlife.

The sharing of past memories during a reading confirms for us here it is a valid connection and for me, past memories were mentioned in every instance when the medium contacted a deceased being. The confirmation of an old memory is called authentication. It may be a memory only you and your deceased person would have recognized and is used to validate the session. The psychics also spoke with the deceased spirit in the present tense and had a conversation with them in response to my questions. When in a conversation with the deceased, there is usually a sharing of photos, memories, and present-day topics are discussed as well. You may discover in your reading that your deceased has witnessed a present-life experience and was present at special ceremony like a graduation or wedding.

My interpretation of these case studies is based on what I observed with some repetition of same-like patterns within each of these scenarios. My thoughts about life after death is based on the premise that information from our existence on earth is never lost when a being dies, but somehow that information is preserved and retained. My next question is naturally directed toward the "how" is information about a deceased person retained after death and in what form does it exist? Could quantum particles capture the deceased person's entire physical, emotional, and historical data in an energy form or wave particles released at the moment of death through something like a Singularity? Is our entire life existence captured after death in a Singularity that entangles itself with the universe?

For example, when **W** found my father it was through an older memory when he existed on earth. As **W** connected with my father, she found him fishing with a cousin. Could it be that as a deceased spirit my father can return to that special fishing spot to re-experience this past moment on earth again? Or was an old memory used by the psychic to validate or authenticate it was really him? Was my father sending the psychic a memory that only I would recognize? I believe these past memories are used as part of the validation process (showing a past event to confirm it was my father). Hence, I knew that the medium had made the right connection. If you choose to pursue a reading, this distinction will help you recognize whether a psychic medium can reach your deceased and is one who has more skills than a tarot card reader.

I am positing the above questions that arose in my mind because of my experience through these connections during these sessions. Each experience with the deceased family/friend seemed to have a bit of the past revealed at the time of the reading. The deceased pets from these connections were always in the present moment during the reading and rarely shared an actual past memory with me. It was only once, with T.C. the cat, who referred to his own past euthanasia, did I have a pet mention a past life experience when on earth. I don't know why there is a distinction between what I experienced with pets versus human spirits.

I only have shared these experiences as how they happened to me precisely as they occurred with the conversations forever engrained in my mind. I am so fortunate to have these experiences, and if another opportunity arises for me to again connect with a deceased friend, family or pet, I will do so readily. The story will be never ending until I cross over and then it will continue hopefully through others researchers reaching out to connect with me on the other side and writing a follow-up book.

Now on to a few scientific theories that may provide some explanation as to how these communications to the deceased are possible. I am summarizing other research studies in the field of quantum physics to determine if science can provide some insight into how these communications are feasible and through what process.

Quantum Theories and Psychic Communication

There are theories surrounding quantum physics and quantum mechanics that posit how information is transmitted, contained and maintained know as quantum theories. I am attempting to raise some questions and find some potential answers as to whether connections to the deceased are scientifically plausible using some quantum theory as a basis. The questions that arise in my mind are the following:

What is the form that information takes about a person's life and how is it retained after death? Can the wave particle principle be applied to after-death existence?

Is that wave particle of a deceased human stored in a quantum wave form? Is this connection that which makes it possible for the deceased to connect to the brain waves of the medium?

Does the speed of light account for the split second connection made when a medium reaches a deceased spirit? Or, is the actual deceased being in a quantum state of wave particles connected through an Opening in consciousness with unique wave particles from the mediums brain being stimulated?

Does this connection between the deceased and the medium, need a portal and is there an actual other dimension? However the deceased energy or their information is stored after death, somehow psychic mediums can reach that energy when they connect using their brain wave pattern.

What is it about the brain wave patterns of the medium that makes it possible to connect to the deceased? What is different in their gray matter development that provides an extra circuitry and can this be seen on a PET scan?

Are the deceased spirits residing right here in the same dimension as we are on earth but just in another form recognizable only through a medium's brainwave capabilities? Is it possible the deceased do visit us and witness our lives here on earth?

Can further research study the actual time during a reading and figure out what quantum physics state is taking place between the medium and the deceased? How is the form from the deceased being interacting with the medium's brain waves?

Definitions of Concepts for Discussion Below

After an attempt to study a few of the quantum theory principles, I tried to place after death information of self into a quantum physics format. Please know I am learning quantum theory at a beginner level and my Ph.D. is in education. I am sorting through this as a researcher using a review of the literature, reading books and trying to put this puzzle together according to my own learning curve.

Does the wave particle theory, combined with quantum physics theories, provide us with a key to how all the information about the deceased is accessed and stored from the brain of the medium?

Do these wave particles contain our earthly physical features, memories, DNA and present after life identity in some dimension that is connected to via a wave particle principle?

How then does the matter (or particles of matter) of the deceased spirit become literally visible during a medium's reading? Note that mediums can see the face and features of the deceased during a reading, so it is not just a brain wave to brain wave connection.

Terms

- <u>Information</u> generally refers to physical data or facts contained in a physical system, e.g. a medical file is data stored in a computer.

Is the information in your mind after death with your brain cells, emotions, physical attributes and life experiences, then become contained in a wave particle that is capable of transmission into a quantum form?

Does storage or retention of information in our DNA remain after death and is placed into a quantum wave particle?

Can life time experiences from our consciousness become a spirit/soul?

Is this information from your consciousness and life time experiences on earth all combined into one simple wave particle?

Is the wave particle accessed in the afterlife a representation of your earthly existence and after death new life ?

- <u>Instance of information</u> refers to the specific <u>instantiation</u> of Information (identity, form or essence) that is associated with the being of *a particular* thing.

Is our spirit's information associated with self (identity, form, and essence) transposed into a particle data form to provide psychics with some type of access to this instance of information?

- <u>Piece of information</u> is a particular fact about a thing's identity or properties, i.e., a portion of its instance.

Hence, the pieces of information about our self with the facts from our former earth existence are then encoded as particular data which is representative of our identity. Is this what the psychic reaches out to connect with when speaking to the deceased spirit through a faster than light connection?

- A pattern of information (or *form*) is the pattern or content of an instance piece of information. Many separate pieces of information may share the same form.

Can it be that those pieces of information about earth self share the same form and they are *copies* of each other stored in a wave particle available to the medium? After death, is this pattern of information compiled into a form that is a copy of our earthly self consistent with our DNA and earthly life experiences? Is this what remains post-death?

- An embodiment of information is the thing whose essence is a given an instance of information.

The total embodiment of information can then possibly be the soul or spirit that remains after death and is representative of the essence of our former self combined with our physical DNA and encoded into a pattern or quantum form.

- A representation of information is defined as an encoding of some pattern of information within some other pattern or instance.

Our spirit becomes a form of encoded data (that is representation of all of self) that retains the prior information from our earth's existence. The memories and experiences is that which is transmitted and accessible during a reading. The present mind of the deceased is in an evolved form of some kind yet consistent with physical features of our earthly self features. When the medium connected to pets and humans alike she could describe their features of face, hair coloring and body type even down to how the person died, e.g. strangling. **W** was able to feel the rope around my cousin's neck when I had not told her it was a suicide. How is this even possible after death and in what form is she feeling and seeing this information?

- An interpretation of information is defined as a decoding of a pattern of information as being a representation of another specific pattern or fact.

A psychic often receives the mental images of what is being verbally exchanged or mentally shared during a reading. So, the interpretation of information by the psychic may be a decoding of the pattern of you in your former self through a quantum form of your DNA. The interpretation of information that is now part of the soul or spirit of one's former memories are combined with a representation of your former physical features in a quantum form.

- A subject of information is defined as the thing that is identified or described by a given instance or piece of information. (Most generally, a thing that is a subject of information could be either abstract or concrete; either mathematical or physical.) As a deceased human or animal, you are the subject of information that is now described by a given piece of information.

- The information highway is a term that represents where information may be stored in space. Is the wave particle of quantum self stored and accessed through time and space in the information highway?

Universe on a T-Shirt: The Quest for the Theory of Everything by Dan Falk, 2004 Arcade Publisher

Six Easy Pieces: Essentials of Physics Explained by Its Most Brilliant Teacher Paperback – March 22, 2011 by Richard P. Feynman (Author), Robert B. Leighton (Author), Matthew Sands (Author)

In summary we take all of the above pieces of information and use it as a reference point. It is possible that after death our quantum data of self is stored in a quantum wave particle and accessible on the information highway. When a psychic's mind connects through wave particles in her brain wave patterns, we as scientists recognize that there are brain waves due to the EEG machine being able to capture those brain waves.

But what about the psychic's mind's capacity makes he/she more capable of accessing or connecting to that information that we ordinary non-psychic brains can do? This topic can be studied further through a combination of research in the neurosciences, consciousness research and quantum physics.

Last question remaining is there even an afterlife or other side where the deceased is stored in some data base on the information life highway we have commonly referred to as heaven?

Summary:

I will take a leap of faith here and try to summarize my thoughts on deceased beings and psychic medium communications. From my own experiences and observations, I believe that once the self (consciousness) is released at death from the body, it transforms into some type of information wave particle which consists of attributes of the physical earthly form in a DNA spiritual or soul mind form of self. The information about the physical self, its life experiences, memories and even its present tense self as a deceased entity is all combined into some quantum substance. Even the conscious thoughts of the deceased are transposed into some type of matter possibly in a subatomic encoded particle that then becomes part of an after death information highway accessible to gifted mediums. Eventually this summary of self in a wave quantum particle is able to be transmitted faster than the speed of light to a psychic during a connection or reading.

When I had my NDE or out of body episode after my car accident, I was not clinically dead. I was, however, able to have a state of consciousness outside my physical form looking down at myself as EMT's arrived on the scene. It was not in a dream like state where you watch or are in the dream as part of the experience it was me observing me outside of my physical self in a consciousness state. That experience has been the single driving force as to why I have pursued understanding that moment in time to the point of exploring mediumship and after life as a topic of research, hence this book! Thank you Dr. Bruce Greyson for your encouragement in helping me acknowledge my NDE .

Somehow mediums connect to both past memories and a present state of the spirit self, which may indicate how all those particles of information are now in one subatomic quantum wave particle. This challenge will bring science to the table to further study the psychic phenomena that is becoming more accepted each day, and combined with quantum theories, may one day be understood.

So, the questions that remain in my mind are as follows:

1) Is it a plan or just part of our natural evolutionary process that some human beings brain waves have this capacity to reach the outer most outer limits of a parallel dimension? Are the psychics, mediums and gifted beings all the future pioneers of our potential mind's capabilities that extends beyond the limits of this physical body? Will we all eventually be connected to both spheres of the brain through the expansion of our brain power to use the full 100% capacity?

2) Is the spirit or soul of the deceased being become an encoded piece of information that leaves the physical body at a precise moment of biological death?

3) Is there a form of encoding of our earth like self which becomes our spirit or soul form that is transposed to a wave like particle?

4) Is the soul a quantum particle that combines with our DNA is what continues on in a physical resemblance form after our death? Is this how the medium then can see the physical features of the deceased entitity?

Is there reincarnation after death? How many lifetimes do we come back before we are offered the final resting place of a heavenly existence? I have not even attempted to touch on this topic but raise it only as it has crossed my mind in trying to understand past lives.

5) Can all of us be psychic? Can one be trained to use that part of their brain that connects with the deceased? Or, does the psychic have a quantum capability outside their actual physical brain structure?

6) If there are truly elements of self that are retained after death, in what format are they retained and where does it get stored that eventually psychics can connect to it?

7) Why are the psychics able to connect with both past memories as well as present interactions with our deceased loved ones when doing a reading?

8) What research can take off from this humble beginning to help us not fear death?

9) Can the use of psychic mediums help people with grief stricken syndromes who mourn the loss of their loved pet or person with coping and moving forward in their lives? Can the psychic connections become a form of a professional service when used in conjunction with a professional counselor or medical professional to guide them through this grief process?

I just am asking the questions, please feel free to consider your own answers and send them to me...<u>drcaruso@hotmail</u>.

All of what I am discussing and suggesting is taken out of and from the actual psychic medium sessions I had experienced. If you are one who is searching for answers, there are many books and articles you can read to further your understanding on this topic. I am just scratching the petri dish here with my one small study. I chose, for the purposes of this book, to remain loyal to my own interpretations and lessons learned from the Other Side (if there really is an Other Side). I hope you have learned some lessons about death and Other Side existence from this book. Thank you for reading it.

When and only when we experience an after death existence, are we then given the answers to the many questions we have pondered since our ancestors first gazed into the stars above.

Blessings from an Empath and a Clairsentient,

Barbara Ann Caruso.

Epilogue

On March 3 I decided to attend a class called in the Meet-Up notice "psychic development". I thought attending such a class would be a way to further my interests in this topic. Well, I had ended up going to the wrong class resulting in my being a part of what was called a "Reader's University" psychic development Meet-Up class. This group was comprised of accomplished mediums which had a wide range of capabilities. On this particular night of the Meet-Up group, there was a practice time for readings with each other to fine tune their skills. I was not aware while sitting in the class where the focus would go, so I just kept quiet being too embarrassed to say I was in the wrong class that night. When asked if I had any experience in medium readings I stated yes, I have done some research for the past twenty years.

The instructor then paired us up and stated, "do a reading and try to focus on 10 identifiers and 20 messages". I was a bit thrown off guard. I then realized that my partner had already started a reading on me and began by telling me "your Father has come through and is sharing how much he is enjoying his new little Grandson". I knew she had no information about my life since I had literally just had walked in the door the same night. I was in shock and thrilled my father had come through but worried I now was to do a medium reading on her?

I sat in total silence trying to decide how to tell the instructor I had made a mistake by coming into this class. I was not a medium and had never done a reading in my life. My spirit guide took charge of me and used my intuition to guide me to close my eyes, and then I said, "please if there is any spirit out there who wants to make contact with my partner here, please, please come through so I don't disappoint her".

With that a woman began communicating with me from somewhere in the universe stating "I am her sister and I need to talk to her". She then shared her feelings, an image with thoughts, as well as a pet she was with on the other side. I was just as blown away as anyone could be that information came through me that had never been guided prior. I had never done a medium reading or even thought I had the gift, ever. I am continuing on with these studies and will work hard at trying to develop my mediumship talents. I have performed ten other readings at the final writing of this book and was accurate on 9 of them.

So, I am sharing this new piece of information with you as I am in total disbelief that I had the capability to reach the spirits from the other side. I believe my experience with the book (and mediums in the stories), prepared me for this new journey in some way. I will be summarizing my next evolution in consciousness development with a follow-up book entitled, "*The Journey of a New Medium: A Surprise Gift from the Universe at Age 65.* Thank you all for trusting in me.

Acknowledgements

To my children, for without you I had no reason to try and become a better person and a more intuitive parent. Thank you for your patience in seeing me through what was a hard topic for you to handle in your own minds. Thank you for all the love and support over the years and for holding me up when I needed you to be my side in this life.

To my parents, who taught me both during their lives and after their deaths, how much there is to living. And that surviving this side of life has the rewards and happiness attainable by evolving to the other side of life. You allowed me to get to know you better by just being who you could be in this life. Then to my greater surprise, you taught me more from your death that I could have ever imagined.

To my sister Sue who has stood by me in this effort to explain my journey and take a leap of faith with her at my side to write this book.

To my pets, who have sustained me minute by minute when no one else was there on those lonely days.

To the many people who have read different versions of this book over the past four years. Special thanks to Konnie, Laurvel, Laura Kay and Sister Sue.

To my friends who have forgiven me and held my hand even when they disliked doing it because they are and will forever be good people.

To all the professionals who taught me that knowledge is a gift in and of itself to pursue for your own blessing and the challenges it brings.

To the mediums and psychics who crossed my path and shared without hesitation their many gifts.

To my patients who have graciously given me their time in life and death teaching me many lessons about courage which helped me write such a book of stories.

To the beauty of nature and Mother Earth who has inspired me in ways that cannot even be explained in words.

To Bruce who encouraged me to continue on with this pursuit and accepted my prior life as okay regardless of what I had done.

And to whatever it is (or whoever it is) that is out there in this life and the afterlife that has seen me through this existence so far. Whether it be religion, god, faith in self or trust in the human condition known as nature, I do not know.

Thank you to the who, whom or whatever it is that is out there that I will meet some day and who will bless me with a presence unlike anything on this side of earth.

For further contact with animal communicators, please go to your state or nationwide directory of animal communicators or psychic mediums. Check out the comments made by others on their website and call the person and interview them before you pay a fee. I paid fees from $30 a session to $450 for a reading, so you need to shop around and find the right person for you.

If you want to contact my newest animal communicator who does not mind me including her email in this book, then write to Jan Reeps at J.Reeps@yahoo.com. I do not have permission to hand out **W**'s information but you can also speak to Terry and Linda Jamison, the Psychic Twins for work with people who have crossed over. They can be reached at their own website under Psychic Twins.

Please take the time to do your research before you connect with a psychic medium for other side communications. Remember that not all psychics can do both animal or human contact so you need to choose which psychic will serve your specific purpose at that time.

CPSIA information can be obtained
at www.ICGtesting.com
Printed in the USA
LVOW12s2100271117
557743LV00001B/171/P